GOD
LOVES
HAITI

Amistad

GOD LOVES HAITI

A NOVEL

DIMITRY ELIAS LÉGER

HarperCollins books may be purchased for educational, business, or sales promotional use. For information, please e-mail the Special Markets Department at SPsales@harpercollins.com.

FIRST EDITION

Designed by William Ruoto

Library of Congress Cataloging-in-Publication Data has been applied for.

ISBN 978-0-06-234813-5

15 16 17 18 19 OV/RRD   10 9 8 7 6 5 4 3 2 1

To my wife, Katarina, and our children,
Sidney and Nina.

And the nine million survivors of the January
2010 earthquake in Haiti, including my cousins
Josette, Fabienne, Reginald, Philippe, Alain, and
Gilbert Léger, and their spouses and children.

After that hot gospeller had leveled all but the
Churched sky,
I wrote the tale by tallow of a city's death by fire;
Under a candle's eye, that smoked in tears, I
Wanted to tell, in more than wax, of faiths that were
        snapped like wire,
All day I walked abroad among the rubbled tales,
Shocked at each wall that stood on the street like a liar;
Loud was the bird-rocked sky, and all the clouds were
        bales
Torn open by looting, and white, in spite of the fire.
By the smoking sea, where Christ walked, I asked, why
Should a man wax tears, when his wooden world fails?
In town, leaves were paper, but the hills were a flock of
        faiths;
To a boy who walked all day, each leaf was a green breath
Rebuilding a love I thought was dead as nails
Blessing the death and the baptism by fire.

    —Derek Walcott, "A City's Death by Fire"

CONTENTS

CONTENTS

PART I

■

When it brushes past,
Death leaves us in a
frenetic state that pushes
us to defy the gods.

—Dany Laferrière, from his Haitian
earthquake memoir, *Tout bouge
autour de moi*

On a five-meter-high pile of gravel where a blink of an eye ago stood a grand airport and a dozen blue-helmeted soldiers having a smoke and a laugh under a cooling shade away from the blistering Caribbean sun, a young woman in a torn dress and one broken high-heeled shoe sat on her elbows and cried. The world had gone white on her in a very unexpected and violent way. Not the tanned white of the skin tones of the Tuscan neighbors she expected to be sipping coffee with after a transatlantic flight. Her entire world had gone white white, and she was still in Port-au-Prince, her eternally godforsaken hometown, confused as hell. A dense cumulus of dust shrouded her eyes. She felt something had gone irrevocably wrong in the universe. Her carefully laid plan to reach a dream so dear to her that she'd sold her soul for it seemed stillborn. She felt like the smallest person in the world. Microscopic. Unmoored and irretrievably lost. She tried to scan the horizon and noticed what was left of the American jet from whose steps she had been rudely ejected a half-minute ago. The jet sat on its back. Wheels-up in the literal sense of the term. She knew that even the finest jet in the world would have trouble taking off from an upside-down position on a runway composed of rubble and fog. She knew this meant she would be stuck in Haiti for a while longer. On a level that shock prevented her from articulating yet, she would try to find honor in this state of affairs, or at least come to see it as an opportunity to restore honor lost. First her head would have to stop throbbing and her ears would have to stop ringing. The goudou-goudou sound must have done this. The rumble would not go away. She felt submerged in it, swallowed up by it. She felt like she was in the belly of a whale, and she was struggling to peer out into the world or find solid footing in its swaying and sloshing. The whale's intestines and pounding heart and lungs pounded hers. Was, was that an earthquake? Only a giant earthquake could shake the ground hard enough to pluck her from an airplane's steps and toss her a hundred meters backward, like a feather, while also taking the airplane and flipping it on its back, like a toy. Did an earthquake destroy the airport and, and, anything else? My God. But she had studied her country's history in school. As best she could tell there was no record of the earth's randomly knocking things about. Granted, she had mainly studied Haiti's art history, particularly works of a spiritual bent, works meant to inspire, heal, and bring folks closer to God. If an artist never painted or sculpted or wrote poetry about an event of the magnitude of a massive earthquake, and the succor of God, Jesus, angels, and saints, in vain, always in vain, after such a ravaging disaster in Haiti, could an earthquake ever have happened here? There had been deadly floods, famines, diseases, hurricanes, civil wars, and invasions in Haiti. That, she knew. All of these events, and every single death, especially the preventable ones, were gut-wrenching, and most were documented one way or another with the creative tools of the day by each era's painters, singers, and poets, and this despite the country's considerable illiteracy rate. The artists almost always tried to celebrate the presence of heaven above by making light and preaching courage in the face of the limits of the human spirit and our fortunes here. It was easy for foreigners and the wealthy who felt safe on their perches to laugh at the believers, Natasha often thought. In the end of times we'd be proven right. Those who laughed now would cry later. After all, it's easier for a rich man . . . blah, blah, blah. My God, am I dead? she thought. Is this hell? Heaven? Could time really have run out on me before I'd painted my Sistine Chapel? Before I'd made things right with Alain, the man I loved but left for a wealthier man?

Natasha was about to blaspheme. She resisted the impulse. Barely. She sensed, on a primitive level, the scale of the rupture in history that had taken place. It frightened her. Her arms and legs and feet were caked with dust, so were her lips, face, and false eyelashes. With no warning, something had transformed her into a Caribbean version of a lava-caked citizen of Pompeii. And she was not alone. The moans of wounded men and women both inside and outside the airport, which had been faint and distant, grew closer and louder. Jesus! Jesus! Jesus! Jesus! they said. *Mon Dieu!* they wailed. A pearly bead of cold sweat trickled down Natasha's temple.

She decided to get off the pile of rubble. She'd read somewhere that earthquakes were known to generate aftershocks. Who knew how long she had been knocked out? Who knew how long she had before the earth betrayed her trust again? She had to get moving before an aftershock transformed her debris pile from a throne to a coffin. Gingerly, Natasha moved her ass down the pile of cement, cheek by cheek, hand by hand, gripping rock and, once, the face of a dead man whose head, judging from how easily it rolled around, had been separated from his body. Finally, she stood on terra firma, whatever that meant at this point. She took stock. Her right knee bled and her left ankle hurt terribly. She still couldn't see beyond two meters in front of her. Her ears still rang with the pounding roar. Like a misting rain, moans, oh-my-gods, and cries for help floated in the air. The voices' glancing touch felt like being pricked by ice. And breathing the heavy air stung Natasha's lungs. When would the itch in her throat go away? The first step she took went off OK. The second step butted on something soft and expiring. A man in a pilot's uniform with half of his head missing stared up at her. As a child, she'd worshiped airplane pilots, as though they were angels, angels who ferried people off her island and into the endless blue sky in hulking metal contraptions that only God had to know how they managed to stay aloft. If these men could foil Haiti's gravity, why couldn't I, Lord?

Now an angel lay dead at her feet. Quietly, Natasha Robert began to weep. She walked on. In tears, she whimpered and limped on. Wearing one shoe. Her destination, unknown. She carefully apologized to each prone person on the ground, whether he or she was dead or alive. The ground was hard to see. The fog was still thick. In truth, she didn't want to look too closely at other people yet. Too often, they were broken up. Their bodies were contorted in ways the body wasn't meant to be. After a while, she couldn't tell for how long she had been walking or where she was. Time seemed to have stood still or shifted in a way she found hard to grasp. She may have walked through the airport and out to the street and around the block and back to the tarmac. Besides moaning and crying for help, she could not hear much else. No sounds of cars, radios, or birds chirping.

A roar overhead caused her to stumble then look to the sky. In the dust-filled air in which birds and even the sun seemed extinct, she saw three planes. Fighter jets. Trailed by plumes of thick black smoke, flags of red, white, and blue stars and stripes plastered on their sides. Flying low, fast, and purposefully, they cleared away the clouds each time they passed. Their sleek bulks emerged. They were magnificent. A second pass. Then a third. Natasha couldn't tell if each trio of planes was the same set or a new one. Suddenly, men clinging to giant white balloons emerged from the jets' trails. Parachutists. Slow like snowflakes, they fell to the ground. No hurry. It was as if they wanted to take in the view from up there. As if they wanted Natasha and the wounded Haitians all around her to bow in awe of them.

Natasha stared at the parachutists with tears streaming down her cheeks. She tried to imagine what Port-au-Prince after an earthquake looked like from their perspective high up in the heavens. Her heart sank with a mixture of terror and embarrassment. Was the city up in flames? Had it sunk into the ocean? Was everyone dead? Was she? If she was dead, what kind of hell was this? How would she know if she was dead or alive? Were those men or angels? Or demons? What was she? How would she know? How would they know? Suppose they didn't know? Suppose they didn't know, then what, man, what? Suppose these men didn't know they were drifting down into hell? Her hell. Foolish, foolish foreigners.

Go away! she found herself screaming while waving at them. Go away! Go away! she kept screaming. The sky was raining men in balloons. Men in little white balloons that got bigger and bigger as they drifted closer and closer to the ground.

Go away! *Go!*

Strong arms soon wrapped themselves around Natasha's waist from behind. A husky voice gently, ever so gently, whispered her name. Natasha, the voice said. Natasha, *ça va*.

Natasha would have none of it. Not even bothering to turn around, she continued to howl at the parachutists.

Go away!

Ça va, the voice said. It's OK.

Go away!

Natasha, it's OK.

Go away!

Shhhhh, *chérie, Calme-toi.*

Go!

Ça va. Ça va. I'm here.

With wild eyes, Natasha turned around to see the face of the man who was rescuing her. It was the president of Haiti, her husband. His clothes were wrinkled and ashy with dust. Yet he looked good . . . not good, but almost. He looked younger than his sixty years, young and fresh. His arms were unusually strong. He held her. He held her. He held her like he never did before. In the past, when he'd try to hold her, she used to wince. In the palace, in his bedroom, anywhere. The few times they'd touched, he was rough or scared. A bundle of nerves. He might have been a virgin before they made love. If she didn't want to protect his pride, she would have asked him. Protecting his pride. That's what she felt her role in his life was to do.

She thought that's why God had brought her into his life. So she could care for a man in need, an old man triple her age who had outgrown the pretense of invincibility men Natasha's age cling to. Natasha could care for someone instead of waiting for a prince charming to take care of her. Lord knew she benefited from the distraction.

Back then, sculpting crucifixes made of trash and assorted debris along Avenue Lamartinière was all that kept her busy. She sculpted morning, noon, and night. It was an obsession. They were pretty and funky, the crucifixes. She liked them and occasionally carved smiles and frowns and, controversially, glee in the dying Jesuses' faces. She sculpted Christ on his cross in different sizes, colors, and materials, and she put them up against walls with the help of strangers and kids. At some locations, folks were inspired to light candles on the ground near her crucifixes. She'd hang back and enjoy the serenity of the scene. Fireflies would come around to dance with the flames. Sometimes people took the crucifixes down overnight. Often they stayed up for days, even weeks. Whenever they disappeared, Natasha hoped they ended up in places of pride, in a family's shack or a villa in the hills. That's how she came to meet the President.

How much do you want for that one? a voice said to her one night. She was standing on the street admiring a particularly cheerful rusty expiring Jesus. This Christ was particularly heavy. The two boys who had been assisting her, Toto and Rodrigue, were exhausted. It was late; the black night's chill drew close. The voice belonged to a dapper little old man leaning against a black Mercedes flanked by four armed men dressed in black and two smaller Asian soldiers wearing blue helmets that were a size too big.

It's not for sale, she said.

Is that a political decision? the old man said. Because there were five of them being sold in front of my house this week.

Really? she said. That's not supposed to happen. They're not for sale. They are gifts to the community. Where do you live?

The National Palace, he said.

Natasha took a step back.

She proved to be a lousy girlfriend and wife, but she tried hard to protect his feelings as best she could. His work was difficult and he was terrible at it. He let her sit in on meetings in his office at the National Palace. And what she saw and heard was not pretty. Just a couple of weeks ago, on January 1, Haitian Independence Day, he had to postpone attending his nation's birthday celebration at the National Cathedral because of a last-minute summons from someone called the special envoy. The special envoy worked on a military base. It was near the national airport, on the road to Tabarre. She never saw such a base before. The entrance was six meters from the street. African and Asian and Latino soldiers wearing blue helmets stood guard in front of the entrance. The base's walls were painted off-white and sky blue. The walls were tall and topped with brand-new and thick barbwire that sparkled in the sun. The creamy blue wall with its crown of metal thorns stretched as far up the street as Natasha could see. Across the street, young men and women stood by booths, selling trinkets and arti-facts of the folksy kind aimed at tourists. White Range Rovers, military buses, and trucks with the letters "U" and "N" painted black on their doors streamed in and out of the base. The base looked like a world unto its own, Natasha thought. How could such a military base with its posh and mysterious ecology hide in plain sight in the middle of Port-au-Prince?

The President had to show ID to get in. Twice. Af-ter the car glided through the hive of military activity, they reached a leafy street. The man they had come to see greeted the President and the first lady near a garden outside his office. He had silver hair, a pointy nose, and white hairy eyebrows reminiscent of Santa Claus, and he wore a tie, a tan suit, and brown shoes. He spoke Spanish to a well-dressed and fresh-faced assistant on his right. He spoke perfect Haitian Creole to the well-dressed and fresh-faced assistant on his left. To the President, he spoke the most *chaleureuse* and mellifluent French. The man was short, shorter than the President; his enthusiastic hand-shake almost made the President lose his balance. After the President introduced Natasha to him, the silver-haired man known as the special envoy bowed courteously. Then he told Natasha to wait outside. The President said nothing. He hadn't said anything since the small humiliations began piling up that morning. He seemed to have nothing to say now. He couldn't even look Natasha in the eyes, so Natasha spoke up.

It's OK, honey, she said. I need some coffee anyway. I think I saw a cafeteria around the corner.

In rapid-fire Spanish, the special envoy ordered one of his assistants to accompany Natasha.

Afterward, during the tardy ride to a ceremony in Fort Dimanche, the gulag-like prison that had emerged as a powerful symbol of the perverted form of justice occasionally practiced on the island, a heavy silence wedged the first couple apart in the presidential car. The President and his wife stared out of their respective windows, as if they were each seeing Port-au-Prince for the first time. Stray dogs, colorful shops, barefoot children, muscular men in finely pressed shirts, big-breasted women in tank tops fanning themselves, ever-present potholes, an ocean-blue sky flecked with rice-white clouds. Natasha had to cling to the handle in the car to survive the car's dips in and out of the giant potholes. With no warning, she began to sing, softly.

Hark! the herald angels sing
Glory to the newborn king

Peace on earth and mercy mild
God and sinners reconciled.

The President laughed.

Very funny, the President said.

So what gifts did the special herald come bearing for our forlorn nation-state?

The President shrugged.

Who was this special envoy anyway?

Our international banker.

What?

Look around you, Natasha. The armored car you're in is a gift from the Canadian government that no local mechanic can maintain, so the special envoy provides the mechanics. You've seen my bodyguards, right?

The President raised his voice, a rare event.

They may be Haitian, but the government doesn't pay their salaries. We can't afford to. The special envoy does. He leads something called the United Nations Mission to Stabilize Haiti.

Stabilize? Stabilize us from what imbalance? How exactly are they stabilizing us?

Only they know. Do you know how many soldiers work for me in the Haitian army currently?

Zero?

Zero. You know how many soldiers with blue helmets the special envoy has working for him currently in his army in your beloved pearl of the Caribbean?

No.

Twelve thousand.

No way! Twelve thousand! Correct me if I'm wrong, but that's a greater armed force—

—than the national police force. I know. We have seven thousand police officers. They are poorly trained, underfinanced, and short fifteen thousand men—

—and women.

And women. Yes. A country this size should have three times more cops than it does, according to the Swedes. They tell me these stats without giving me the resources to change the situation, knowing full well we can't generate the resources on our own. For example, the international community took our army away from us years ago.

Why can't we have a new one?

The President got irritated.

We can't, OK? We can't.

Natasha grew irritated too. The car had rumbled off Boulevard Toussaint Louverture and into the Carrefour Trois Mains roundabout. She stared at the tips of the fingers on the golden statue of big hands holding a globe in the wan morning sun. The fingers were rotten with rust.

The President continued his lament.

Meanwhile, the special envoy back there has an army, a good one too. With all their small Asians, skinny Africans, and bronzing Brazilians, these blue helmets may look like a ragtag outfit. But do not underestimate them. They benefit from state-of-the-art facilities and weapons.

Stuff Haitian soldiers couldn't dream of. Most of them have seen action in some of the worst wars around the world, Sudan, Iraq, Afghanistan, Congo.

So now they're in big bad Haiti? Doing what? Defending us against a potential invasion of transforming warrior robot cars? Natasha sucked her teeth. You're too impressed by these foreigners and their guns and money, she said. You're not scared of them, are you?

Lower your voice, he said.

You are scared!

Let it go.

Lord have mercy, why are you scared of these people?

You don't know what you're talking, Natasha. You don't know these people.

What's to know? They spend more money on weapons than food and medicine. That says all I need to know about them. After that, what makes them special? They put their pants on one leg at a time like us. They bleed like us. Get hungry like us. One thing you have that they don't is that you are Haitian and they are not. You were democratically elected to lead this country. Twice!

You don't know what they can do, the President whispered. You don't know what they have done. You just don't know.

What don't I know?

You just don't know.

Well, tell me then.

You just don't know, he said.

Then the President began weeping. Oh Lord, Natasha thought. He had his back turned to her. The limo was dark. She noticed the smell of vanilla for the first time. Nice move, driver's wife, she thought. The President was looking at his hands. His head hung low. For once, Natasha didn't judge the old man or calibrate how she should react to him. She did what felt natural. She slid across the seat in the back of the limo and she hugged him. He embraced her with the grip of a drowning man, tearing her blouse a little. The President sobbed like a child on her shoulders. Fat tears streamed from his eyes and down her back. They gave her chills.

Sweetheart, she said, if I agree to marry you, can we leave for Italy, like we've talked about, as quickly as possible?

Yes, he said, after a pause. Thus, the rescued became the savior.

Are you sure you can walk away from the presidency?

Yes, he said. It's just a job. It's not like it was a vocation, like you and your art. This country took every ounce of everything I have for sixty years. It's past time I left it to the young turks who want to run it so badly. Like that Destiné boy.

Natasha closed her eyes. She held on to her husband with both hands. Dug her nails into his back. Her heart palpitated like a leaf in a hurricane. Alain, she thought. She bit into the President's shoulder. What will I tell Alain?

Less than two weeks later, the apocalypse landed on Haiti. Alain Destiné, at first, was the furthest thing from Natasha's mind. No man ever held Natasha as firmly as the President held her on the tarmac after the earthquake. Natasha had never before found herself needing to be held so much in her life. She stood in a white fog under a sad sun on a shattered airport's tarmac on a dog of an evening. She couldn't see. She couldn't hear. She couldn't understand what had happened, why everyone around her was dead or broken or bleeding. Or where her future went. She felt as though God had swept down and withdrawn all love from around her. She felt cold, man. Freezing. But here was this man, her husband, the weakest man she'd ever met. He was keeping her upright because her legs were failing her. He seemed the picture of good health. His arms felt firm, like bent steel, around her waist. The man she believed was a big baby with a job that was way too big for him was, in her most freaked-out hour, strong and confident and capable of holding her up, nursing her toward feeling confident she would actually live to find out what happened to the world.

You're alive, Natasha babbled. You're alive!

Yes, the President said, and not the worst for wear either, all things considered. Come on. You're hurt. We have to get your injuries checked out.

With alert eyes, a becalmed Natasha sat on a stretcher and drank slowly from a bottle of water. A cheery blond medic worked on her bleeding knee and twisted ankle. Is this OK? he said very politely each time before he touched her knee. She barely spoke or understood English, but she could get his drift and nodded. A scene developed around her as a pink dusk fell on Port-au-Prince. Americans. They were everywhere. They were blond, or of African descent; some of them even were women. In her short time in the art world in Port-au-Prince, she'd already learned to tell the difference between Americans and Europeans, no matter their ethnic origin. They walked into rooms differently and made eye contact differently when they spoke, especially to locals like her. These were definitely Americans, and they were fluttering down from the sky, like dollar bills in her dreams of massive wealth. The soldiers, and these were definitely military personnel, wore airplanes on their uniforms and jumpsuits. They surrounded the President, making presentations, explaining action plans. There was a group hunched over laptops. They spoke to the heavens. They guided airplanes, helping them find landing patches on the ruined tarmac. There seemed to be a backlog of airplanes trying to land in Haiti. This scared her. She bit her lower lip.

Did, did I hurt you, ma'am?

It was the medic. So cheerful.

Why, she said, Why are all these planes coming here? What happened? Natasha pointed to the sky. A smoky black curtain of night had fallen. You could hear the drone of the planes' engines. You could see the blinking red lights as some of them weaved between clouds. You couldn't see them, though. You felt them. You felt them in your bones.

That's help, cheerful medic said.

Seeing the alarm in her eyes, happy medic softened his voice. There was an earthquake, he said. He was about her age, but he tried to speak to her like one would speak to a child. She didn't like him.

We estimate the earthquake may have destroyed over seventy percent of the buildings in Port-au-Prince, he said. The epicenter was near Carrefour and Léogâne, which are now completely destroyed. The earthquake measured seven point zero on the Richter scale. The force was unheard of for the capital city of a country, particularly a country as small and densely populated as Haiti. We're afraid thousands of people may have died. Most buildings were flattened or damaged. Even the National Palace and the cathedral. I'm so sorry. We only have aerial and satellite shots of the city so far. In the coming days, hopefully things will reveal themselves to be better than we fear.

The National Palace? she thought, feeling a sharp pinprick in her heart. Alain! She had bid her ex-lover a final farewell in her room in the National Palace that morning, leaving him trapped and helpless. At once, Natasha felt every ounce of energy leave her body. Dante was wrong, she thought. This is what hell is like. In hell, you're alive but everyone and everything that you love is dead and destroyed, and you don't know what to do or say. Dante didn't get it. You had to die or receive this kind of news to truly glimpse hell. Hell to the exiled Florentine was mere homesickness. Hell, Dante, is the physical destruction of your entire hometown, and the death of your lover by your own hands. Natasha, who fancied herself a capable artist in the best traditions of Florence, suddenly could not imagine how art or poetry could come from people who even once in their lives felt the blackness of death so completely envelop them. It's like being buried alive. Thousands dead. Alain! She wiggled some toes to make sure she was still alive.

She was,

Merde.

On the bright side, the medic continued, taking a break from dressing her wounded legs, we're here.

The bright side!

He waved his hand to show off the buzzing activity around them. An army base had spontaneously developed near the debris of the national airport. On the horizon of the black sky, a swarm of helicopters, airplanes, and parachutists choked off views of the emerging silver moon. On the ground, things felt lively, even chipper. Soldiers built tents of various sizes, including a large cafeteria, which reminded Natasha how hungry she was. There were civilians in cargo pants and, oddly, hiking boots and even sandals. Their pale faces ranged from middle-aged to impossibly young. They looked scruffy, bespectacled, and keen. Humanitarian aid workers. Had to be. The rest of the foreigners seemed to be mostly military. The military men and women were unlike the soldiers Natasha was accustomed to seeing around town. For one, they sometimes wore non-combat uniforms and carried small guns. They were bright-eyed, open, and friendly while going about their work. This operation seemed to involve a lot of talking into headsets and cell phones and staring at bright laptop screens. Energetic medics fanned out to help the bleeding Haitians who walked on hands, bellies, and feet toward them like believers to John the Baptist on the river Jordan.

The sight that soon riveted Natasha was that of her husband, the President, leading. Of all things. In the middle of a circle of the most grizzled members of the international rescuers, the diminutive fat man seemed to be in charge. Under the yellow lights of military trucks and ambulances, he was absorbing information from engineers and air force commanders and firemen with brandnew tool belts. He kept a thoughtful hand on his chin. He fired questions back at them with orders, directions, and times for follow-up meetings. When he was done talking, the men—and they were all men, a fact that saddened Natasha—dispersed briskly, checking their watches. They seemed keen on doing a good job for Haiti after a disaster whose proportions Natasha found hard to grasp and difficult to even imagine without going glassy-eyed to the point of feeling faint and sleepy.

Are you OK? the medic at her feet said.

She'd forgotten he was there.

That's my husband, she said, pointing to the President, a bit surprised at how easy it was for her to utter those words for the first time. Was that pride in your voice, Nat? she thought. Is it because the President looked and behaved like he had grown a foot taller since disaster struck? Like he was the president of a nation, a leader of free men and women and children in need of wise leadership? She remembered stories of girlfriends who were actually annoyed after a boyfriend acquired a shot of self-confidence from a success or an event unrelated to being with them. Pity had been Natasha's default mode for men and their delusions of control . . . until today.

I know, the medic said.

You know what? she said.

I knew he was your husband.

Stop, she said.

What, did I say something wrong?

No, no, you've done a good job. I feel fine. Why don't you go help that lady over there with the baby? I need to go talk to my husband, if you don't mind.

D'accord, he said in French to please her.

It worked.

The President stood alone in a spotlight from trucks and ambulances, lights that had been turned into makeshift streetlights. He was on a new phone. The deep creases in his furrowed brow suggested he was receiving bad news. In the past, during these moments, he would stand with his back bent and a pleading look on his face, a cue for Natasha or Reginald, his assistant, to have at the ready a soft chair for him to sit on and a stiff glass of rum for fortification as soon as he got off the phone. They were meant to help refill his spirit, since the effort of not having answers in the face of the enormous problems around him taxed his intellectual and emotional capabilities. Oh, *ce peuple*, he would say afterward, *Ils me laissent à bout de force.*

Tonight, he stood erect while wearing a broken watch, one suede loafer, and a ruined suit jacket with only one sleeve left. Not to mention having what looked like a broken jaw. He stood erect but his face and spirit radiated empathy. Compassion. Generosity. Why now? Finding the courage gene at the one moment in his life when he would be forgiven for not having any. Who was this man? Natasha thought, while limping toward him.

His lined yet newly youthful brown face broke out in a wide smile when he turned to her. *Mon amour*, he said, before wrapping her warmly in his arms. He was calm and steady, and he hugged her exactly how she needed to be hugged. She let herself go like a basket case again.

What are we going to do? she asked him once her sobbing had slowed to a stream. For the first time in her driven and imaginative young life, she really had no idea what to do next. We sleep, he said. Tomorrow will be a better day. It has no choice.

He led her by hand to their new home, a tent on the tarmac. It was military green, about two by four square meters. It featured a cot, a foldable chair, and a table with a small lamp. I'll sleep on the floor, the President said. The pre-earthquake President would have tried to sleep on the cot with her or have made a lame joke about having to give up the cot. This new President sat her down on the cot gently. When he tried to pull away from her, she tugged at him, and, instead, he sat close to her. Natasha held on to the arm he had around her.

Reginald is dead, he said.

Natasha stared at the floor of their tent. It was made of the same plastic material as the walls. The tent's lamp worked. How'd that happen? Her eyes trailed all the cables running through the tent. There were quite a few.

Marcel, Marie-José, François, Philippe, Jean-Yves, Yves-Antoine, Elias, all dead. Dozens of party members, dead. For Jean-Francois, it was almost worse. The twins died with their mother. The school walls crushed their car as they prepared to drive away. My house is gone. No one can find mother.

Outside, all the other tents around them had yet to go dark. The Americans were too busy to sleep yet. There was a buzz worthy of the Marché de Fer on a Saturday morning—construction machines drilling, orders being given, yes-sirs being answered. The President continued: You can almost hear all the wailing going on in the country, can't you? Everyone, absolutely everyone, on the island lost something today. I bet the diasporas are going mad with worry.

You believe they know already? Natasha said.

For sure, the President said. In the first hour, it felt like I spoke to more journalists than I did military rescue personnel. It felt like the country now has more foreign journalists and aid workers alive and kicking in it than healthy Haitians.

Healthy Haitians? What the hell are those? I've been looking for that breed for over twenty years. I thought they were extinct. Didn't the Duvaliers kill them all off?

No, I think it was the Americans.

Yes, the Americans. During the occupation, right? Fucking Americans. What else can we blame them for?

The earthquake?

Yes, the fucking earthquake. How do you think they caused it? The testing of new nuclear bombs by American submarines operating in the bottom of the Caribbean Sea

Good one. In fact, it wasn't even an earthquake. It was some new-style nuclear bomb experiment. They were aiming for Venezuela and the missile landed here.

Can't get nothing right, those Americans.

Yeah. But they're great at racking up civilian casualties, though. You gotta give them that.

We mustn't make light.

You're right. It's too early.

Yes, too early. Think about all those people out there who lost their homes. They don't have tents.

Is it too early to think about sex?

Sex?

You know, sex. Birds and bees. Sweat. Screaming at the end. I heard sex could be useful during national emergencies.

Emergency sex?

Yes. The idea came in the president's manual. I think it may actually be a clause in the constitution.

It's one of the Ten Commandments too.

Could be. You're my connection to the divine. If you say it is, then it must be so.

It's the eleventh commandment. It was in the small fine print that no one bothers to read. God slid that in there past us.

No pun intended?

No pun intended!

All Haitians are dead, and there's only us left. What to do?

Commence repopulating?

Commence repopulating. Immediately.

Hey, be careful with the legs. Fragile merchandise. Handle with care.

Be careful with my head. Very tender.

Which one?

They giggled. They embraced. They fell asleep. The President and his wife did not make love that evening.

WELCOME TO PLACE PIGEON

The morning after the earthquake, to the surprise of most folks in Haiti and around the world, the sun rose over Haiti, as it had since the dawn of time. Pulsing, brilliant, and warm, it shone over the land like glorious yellow candlelight with a special affection for Caribbean islands. The sun over Haiti the day after the earthquake lodged in a clear sky so blue the Caribbean Sea seemed to reach up and merge with it. The air, too, retained its customary light fragrance. The freshness of the air inspired roosters to sing their hearts out, and sing they did that morning, determinedly, robustly, and with pride. The island was still above water, and palm trees felt cool enough about this state of affairs to cock their long, leafy crowns just so. The morning brought rising heat. And the warming of the ground beneath his buttocks spurred Alain Destiné into another attempt at holding on to his consciousness. Squinting and rubbing his eyes, Alain briefly ignored the sharp pain spreading throughout his body to take in his surprising location: one of the parks across the street from the National Palace. Alain saw his car. To his astonishment, the car hung about ten meters in the air, impaled on the statue of a woman holding a pair of pigeons. The statue gave the park its name, Place Pigeon. Pigeons liked the homage and congregated there regularly en masse. Before the park became the site of his seemingly impending doom, Alain had liked Place Pigeon too. Back when he dated unmarried women, the young bachelor took dates on strolls through this park after an evening at the movies at Le Capitol, the nearby theater. The couple would be wearing their Sunday best and talking breathlessly about the baroque drama of the kung fu films they'd seen. Young lovers in Port-au-Prince had been doing so since his father's and his grandfather's eras. Following tradition always made Alain happy. He had a lifelong thing for Haitian society's old-world notions of honor and gallantry. You're so old-fashioned for a boy, the women of various ages he courted often told him. He knew he had them once they said that. For women, he'd learned at a precocious age, liked to be wicked with boys their parents and the rest of the world found nonthreatening.

Still, Alain wished he were anywhere else on earth than Place Pigeon at that moment. A creak and a soft tilt downward from the Chevy suspended in the sky snapped Alain's attention to the very real possibility of his sudden death. More daydreaming and you're dead, Alain, and suicides aren't allowed into heaven, remember? Blotchy red against the vast blue sky, the car seesawed casually. Under the car's shadow, Alain tried to calculate how much time he had to crawl away before a breeze caused his car to fall on his head. Not much, he correctly concluded, especially considering that Alain and the car had likely been in their respective positions since the previous evening. Death was imminent. Shit. Death was imminent yesterday afternoon too, Alain thought. What in God's name happened? One minute I'm driving slowly on rue St. Honoré, and the next minute, buildings started tumbling on people as if they were made of cards. The car turned into a flying carpet, and then, then . . . I'm waking up in a park, like a bum, hurt in places I didn't know my body had, and the car is still in the air, but now suspended from above as if it were passing judgment on my life.

Judging the man-sized hole in the windshield, Alain at least understood how he came to be separated from the car. Time to move your ass, man, Alain thought. Then he discovered he could not move his legs. Alain couldn't even feel his legs. *Merde*, he thought. Must worry about that later. After crossing himself, he dug his fingers as deeply as he could into the ground, then he pushed himself backward with all his strength. Grunting up spittle, which dribbled down his suit, shirt, and his pants, Alain pushed and pushed, but he did not move one inch. A light breeze. In the air, the car squealed. Its fender aimed squarely at Alain's groin, a prelude to one of the worst fender benders a man could imagine. Come on, Alain, he said. *Allez*. Push yourself, man. Alain grunted. *Bouge ton cul*. You can do this. Alain pushed. He pushed and pushed and pushed some more. Small progress: the car's fender now aimed for his knees. Before he could push again, a stronger wind swept through Place Pigeon, and the Chevy came tumbling down from the hands of the statue. Mother of Christ! Alain said. *No! No! No! No!* he screamed. The car landed with a thud and sprayed metal and glass in a shriek of twisting steel. Fortunately for Alain, terror had given him the last burst of strength he needed, and he had used it well, pushing himself out of harm's way, a full three meters from where the car crash-landed. Alain had moved so fast that his ass burned, a trail of dust hovered in the air. Out of breath and coughing, Alain stared at the car with fright. No, he said one more time. Then he passed out.

Some time later, the sour scent of his own piss, like smelling salts, startled Alain awake. How long had he been out? Clearly not long enough for the events of the past dozen or so hours to disappear in a nightmare's blur and return him to his normal and, all things considered, not terrible life. In that life, he'd lost the woman he loved to a rich old man, but at least his legs were functional, which gave him a decent shot at running after her and winning her back. In that life, his city had a ground you could run on and not feel like running from. Now the world around him was filled with horror. Herds of people had settled on every patch of available dirt in the park. Women, men, and children, all looking hysterical and in pain, like they, too, had had recent and unusual encounters with death. Their own shadows made them nervous. They were jumpy and kept looking up at the sky or over their shoulders, as if they feared an attack, as if the sky might decide to fall on their heads or the ground might turn into quicksand. Most of those heads already nursed garish injuries. Most shoulders sported bleeding gashes mixed with gravel or dirt. Or was that cement? As if the arms had been used to protect their owners from falling objects. Their eyes now darted to and fro, as if, having barely survived nearly getting buried alive, every sense yearned for connections to community and humanity. The people clutched and touched everyone near. Alain guessed they touched each other because they needed help shaking off the shock of whatever had happened that seemed to have stripped them of everything save their lives. I did it, their faces said. My God, we did it. Survival needed constant affirmation. Alain had seen this look before. It was after a runaway truck at a carnival sent a crowd running for cover. He was a small boy. The mob reached him when they ran out of steam. His father had him fetch them water, out of his customary generosity. People took the water from Alain without looking and drank while looking over their shoulders in the direction of the danger they had just fled. Some of those survivors were so distracted they missed their mouths while trying to drink the water. They missed his tray when they tried to put the cups down.

These disaster survivors were different. They looked like survivors of an avalanche, and Alain was in no position to help them. He was one of them and felt exactly how they felt. Fucked-up and scared out of his wits. Terrified of what unexpected shit the next second of life could bring. From his seat on the ground, Alain strained to see the world beyond the mob of survivors. A couple hundred of them already filled the park. Unable to stand, he saw only jumbles of limping legs and feet and groins and white dust-covered clothes and swollen, sad faces. On his right, beyond the fence and across the street, Alain took a look at the National Palace. The two-story domed manse had been reduced to one story. The dome was gone, caved into the building. The memory of witnessing the revered building's destruction while his car flew through the sky came back to him. He broke out in sweat and felt the return of the now familiar—hopefully not permanent—terror run through his body. What force could do that, casually destroy one of the biggest buildings in the country and throw cars into the air like leaves? A nuclear bomb? On Port-au-Prince? No, Alain had read John Hersey's *Hiroshima* at university. Even if he and these people had managed to survive being at ground zero of a nuclear explosion, their bodies and the city would either be on fire or coping with burn wounds. The very air around them would still be burning. The air would be thick with radiation and rendered invisible and unbreathable by lingering clouds. In short, we'd be dead. And the sun wouldn't have come out so quickly. So brightly. So damn perkily. Fucking Caribbean sun. Besides, today's nuclear bombs were stronger than Hiroshima's. If one landed here, or anywhere on Hispaniola, even by accident, it likely would have sunk the island. Today, Haiti, like man since his first encounter with death, persevered. Worn, but still here. Heads above water. Barely. What else could . . . an earthquake?

Oh my God, an earthquake. It was an earthquake! Had to be. But there's no history of earthquakes in Haiti. None whatsoever. His parents, grandparents, and great-grandparents never mentioned it. And picking apart the nation's colorful, sorrowful, and thrilling history is all Haitians do. It's a sport, the fucking national pastime. History is all we have to take pride in, since our greatest achievement occurred in 1804, and we hadn't contributed fuck-all to humanity in the intervening two centuries save a few good books and paintings. Dining out on the heroes of independence of 1804 allowed Haitians to overlook the mess we made of the present. No one would have overlooked a major earthquake in this society's, and indeed the world's, constant search for proof that Haitians are or aren't God's children, put on one of earth's most beautiful corners to suffer absurd streams of misfortune. But how else could Alain explain the buildings he saw falling over like dominos on rue St. Honoré? And all these people sporting injuries that could come only from falling objects? Gashes and wounds on their heads, shoulders, and arms, arms that were probably used in futile attempts to protect themselves from falling debris, houses, trees, and . . . cars.

Fuck. An earthquake hit Port-au-Prince! Must have been huge. My God, the city is too crowded. Its houses too poorly built. Too much liberal use of cement everywhere. Too-lax building safety regulations. Our government is too ill equipped! Too few hospitals, doctors, nurses, beds, and even ambulances. Fuck. My Lord, how, how could You allow this to happen? *Here and now?* Three million people are said to live here, but we all know the number is closer to five million. Fuck. Fuuuuuuuuuck. God, how could You? What father does that to . . .

Hey!

Someone had walked quietly up to Alain and poked him in the head with a stick. It was a boy. A naked boy of about six years old was staring at him with the biggest, brownest, and softest honey-chocolate-colored eyes Alain had ever seen. The reflection of himself he saw in the boy's eyes gave Alain pause. He looked like shit. Dirty, swollen face. Hair askew. Wounded and mangy, like roadkill. He looked scared and crazy. In desperate need for medical attention. The child, meanwhile, wore preternatural calm. As if he didn't realize he was nude and covered with dried mud, the child looked at Alain with familiarity and tenderness.

I was taking a bath, the boy said. Maman was telling me a story about why I should stop playing with the big boys across the street. Then goudou-goudou came. It was loud. I couldn't hear her voice anymore. I couldn't hear anything but goudou-goudou, goudou-goudou, goudou-goudou. The room rocked back and forth, back and forth. Mummy wanted to hug me. Then the ceiling came crashing down on her.

The boy mimicked a roof caving in. Mother disappeared, he said. The roof fell on her. In midsentence, she disappeared. All of her except her hands. It was strange: her fingers continued to stroke my shoulder. I pulled her hand away and climbed out of the bathtub and walked around the pile of debris that filled the room. I apologized to Maman for walking over her. After one last look to see if she would climb out of the pile of cement—don't laugh; you don't know how strong my mother was—I walked out of the house through a small hole of light where the front door used to be.

Why are you telling me all this, little boy? Alain said. I feel bad for you. I really do, but, as you can see, I got my own problems.

The pain in Alain's legs had sizzled up his back and neck and grown sharp and overwhelming once his adrenaline shock had worn off. Alain felt that the boy's lament was distracting him from the more fun preoccupation of suckling the black rage and pain exploding in his head, blurring his vision and emptying his usual glass-half-full disposition. He was angry with God for allowing nature to strike Haiti with such tragedy. The blasphemy felt good. It crept hrough Alain's physical pain like water moving through a living room from an overflowing toilet. He was determined to not let this angelic little orphan dull his rage.

The boy hadn't moved an inch. He just stared at Alain with kindness.

Leave me alone, Alain said. I got my own problems.

The boy pretended not to hear him and continued his story. I crawled through the debris that blocked my front door, the boy said. The dark tunnel seemed to be the only way out of the house. I felt like I was in a Kirikou story. I crawled through the tunnel until I got to the street. There wasn't much street left, as the house across the street, one of the biggest in Fort National, had collapsed into a pile of rubble onto the street as well. Every house on our block had done the same.

I don't know what to tell you, son.

There was white dust everywhere. The goudou-goudou sound disappeared. The sounds I heard on the street were of people crying. They were crying for help. They were buried, they said. Could someone help please? they screamed. Some of the people crying were kids. I recognized the voices of some of my friends. Their voices were brightest and went silent quickest.

How did you end up here? Alain said. What's your name anyway?

Xavier. A crowd of survivors swept me up as they clambered up and down and through the mountain of debris that had replaced the street. They were quiet. They were hurt. They shuffled more than walked. Like zombies are said to. They scared me. But I joined their stream and followed. I didn't want to be alone. The man leading them said he would find us help. His name was Philippe. He found us this park. We walked only two blocks or so. I'm not sure. I can't count too well yet. The wounded were too hurt to walk or be carried any further. So we stopped here.

So this crippled crew is supposed to take care of you? Where are your other relatives?

I only had a grandmother and a sister besides my mother. She was a baby. They were sleeping in the room that collapsed on my mother. The roof may have caved in on them before bringing the house down on my mother. Somehow sparing me.

Somehow sparing you. I got spared too. Ain't we a pair of pretty motherfuckers. Look at us. I can't walk and you're naked with no family. I tell you, the dead are the lucky ones.

Don't say that.

They don't have to deal with this mess. Look around you, boy. The dead won't get to see the city, the palace, and their brothers and sisters looking so broken.

Don't say that!

The child's shriek startled Alain and, seemingly, all of

beleaguered Port-au-Prince, even the somnolent pigeons. The cry shattered the stiff air and mournful atmosphere of the park. The dazed crowd from Fort National around Alain and Xavier consisted of traumatized and wounded people who sat so still with wide, vacant eyes you could hardly separate the living from the dead. The child's scream almost stirred them. Almost.

I'm sorry, Alain said to the child, opening his arm, the good one, the one that didn't feel like it wanted to secede from his body. The boy hugged him.

As if out of thin air, three humanitarian aid workers appeared in the middle of the park turned earthquake refugee camp. They stood between the upside-down Chevy, a ragged pile of survivors, and Alain and Xavier. They were two men and a woman. They wore khaki pants, preposterous can-do attitudes, and shirts and vests featuring large red crosses. Two of them carried medical aid kits. Excitedly, the boy touched Alain's leg and said, I told you help was coming! I told you!

After the boy ran off to join the crowd slowly forming around the aid workers, Alain Destiné discovered a familiar sensation. He felt his legs. He. Felt. His. Legs. He knew he might be able to walk again. He looked at the sky, then he looked at the hopping, giddy boy, then he looked at his legs. The boy turned around and winked at him. Again Alain looked at the boy, then he looked at the sky, and then he looked at his legs. The sky was an unmoved blanket of light blue with nary a cloud in sight. He tried to wiggle his toes, and the little bastards actually wiggled. The smile he smiled started from deep inside him before flowing through his face. His vision was blurred by a mix of tears and sweat. His chapped and dry lips cracked from stretching into a smile for the first time in a long time. Alain closed his eyes and tried to calm his heart. I still don't forgive You, he said. But this is not a bad way to start Your comeback in my good graces.

Opening his eyes, Alain saw the boy staring right back at him, smiling. Whoa, he said. The boy was clothed. He wore a white T-shirt emblazoned with a big red cross and the word "Haiti" written in a cheerful script, and khaki shorts. Yellow-and-green sandals with a small Brazilian flag shod his feet. He carried a lollipop and had a Band-Aid on his right forearm. Alain felt bad for never having noticed the boy's injuries. Xavier, he said, my, don't you clean up nicely.

Around them a few other children, dressed like Xavier, chased a plastic blue-and-white soccer ball in the little bit of free space still available. They did so quietly, as if still warming to the concept of fun in their strange new world. They seemed to not to want to disturb their shell-shocked neighbors and relatives. Death had taken ownership of the city in one fell swoop. The kids rightly suspected she would not relinquish her grip gently. To fight for release from her cruel stroke, these coming days would take more energy than Alain had. He just wanted to go home, take a bath, and sleep. Maybe forever. That would be nice.

We need your help, Xavier said. The people who came to help speak only English. No one else from Fort National speaks it well enough to follow them. Philippe, my neighbor who led us here, can't translate what they're saying. Since you speak good English, I told them you could translate for us.

How did the boy know I spoke English? Alain thought. Not that the question mattered much. He was tired. His first and only instinct at the moment was to recoil from the world around him. He wanted nothing more than to jump into a car and hurry to his father's house on Place Boyer and climb into his bed and lie there for a month or a year or two. That his car lay on its back and his house could be in the same shape bothered him, but not more than the exhaustion of looking so many hurt people in the face.

Everything's going to be all right, the boy said again, as if reading his mind. Come with me.

The boy pulled Alain's arms like he expected Alain to have the ability to get up and stand on his own two feet with no problem. Alain stood on his two feet with no problem. *Merci*, Alain whispered.

De rien, the boy said. *Viens*.

Allowing himself to be tugged toward the three humanitarians and their crowd of eager beneficiaries, Alain Destiné stuck out his square jaw, flashed his battle-tested negotiator's grin, and soon began shaking hands with a businessman's winning handshake. Martin, Mariana, and Adam, they were doctors, two Canadians and a Peruvian. While bandaging and dispensing painkillers to the group of earthquake victims still mobile enough to come to them, they briefed Alain on Haiti's status. Seven-point-two magnitude earthquake, thousands dead, most of Port-au-Prince and Léogâne destroyed. As Alain tried to digest the news, locals pressed him to tell the doctors to come help a dying child or parent or sibling or neighbor lying about somewhere around the park or in the rubbled city beyond it. In the middle of the action, tugged at all sides, feeling useful, Alain briefly felt a surge of his old adrenaline. But the effort was tough. The back of his neck began to sweat. The noon sun and heat felt like they were closing in on him. The smell of mass deaths, plangent and sour, started to fill the park, sapping him. Alain had to shake hands with his left hand because the right one was still no good and hurting. Keeping the boy close to him, Alain steadied himself. As had happened to him whenever his self-esteem perked up, he found himself thinking of Natasha.

Where are you, baby? You should be here, he thought.

For the first time since the earthquake, he thought of the woman he loved, the same woman who, when they last saw each other, seemingly an eternity ago, locked him in a closet and said good-bye to him. It was never meant to be for us, was it? Alain could now begin to concede.

Dr. Mariana was the least Latina-looking Mariana Alain had ever met. She had red hair, green eyes, freckles, and a nose too big for her face. She turned out to be the leader, or at least the spokesperson, of this troika of saviors. They came from the Canadian Red Cross; they were student trainees on a mission of observation only, but the scale of the disaster had forced them into duty. She said there indeed had been earthquake. In turn, Alain played translator, relaying the information to the crowd as loudly as he could. They nodded at the news with no emotion. An earthquake?! Of course! Only God could test us like that, their faces said. Fuck God, Alain thought. Xavier looked up at him, again, as if he'd read his mind, as if to tell him that resistance was futile. The earthquake was massive and unprecedented, Mariana said. The earthquake originated somewhere between Carrefour and Léogâne and caused extensive damage, destroying most homes. Even the United Nations lost its headquarters and dozens of staffers. The event made headlines around the world, and the world had responded with an outpouring of sympathy and support for Haiti. Billions of dollars were being gathered. An unprecedented collaboration between American military forces and charities from everywhere had been working all through the night to stabilize the situation and bring medical and other aid to everyone. The only reason Marianna and her colleagues were already in place was because they were in town attending a workshop at the Canadian Embassy when the earthquake struck. After a night of caution, they came out first thing in the morning to do reconnaissance for a damage assessment report.

As if she anticipated his next question, Mariana announced that the President was alive. The plane he was to take at the time of the earthquake was destroyed, and the President was bruised but alive and kicking. He was working closely with the United Nations and the international community in a temporary office near the airport to get help to Haiti as quickly as possible. And the first lady? Alain asked. Everyone looked at him like he was crazy, like, Where did that question come from? Alain squeezed Xavier's shoulder during the silence that preceded Mariana's answer. No news on the first lady, Mariana said. *Pauvre diable*, an elderly woman standing next to Alain said.

Alain went light-headed and his knees buckled. Little Xavier held him up until a couple of older guys noticed and came to help. To everyone's surprise, Alain pulled himself out of his fainting spell. Fine, he said to no one in particular, let's be grateful for what we still have. Our president is alive and doing his part. Let's do our part.

He ordered the able to help the weak stand and form a line to receive basic care from the nice Canadians. More Canadians came, and they came with the good stuff. For lunch, the refugees ate crackers and drank a sip of water. When dinnertime came, they ate the same things. Be grateful, Alain said to everyone as he helped distribute the food. Be grateful.

Over the next couple of weeks, Alain slept a dreamless two to three hours a night on a military-gray cloth covering a piece of cardboard in a tent pitched on a grassy patch in the park. After the blue embers of dawn filtered through the tent's seams, he sprang up, sat, and listened to the sounds of the new world he had come to inhabit in Park Pigeon. A dog sniffing about. The clang and hiss of a giant pot being cleaned by Yanick, the camp's designated chef. The soft hiss of a child pissing. The boy Xavier had refused to stray more than a meter away from Alain since they'd met. Pre-earthquake, Alain had greeted new days with as many push-ups and sit-ups as he could muster no matter where he was. Today, he barely had enough energy to keep his eyes open. One of his legs was broken and without the benefit of casts was healing in all sorts of ugly shapes. His washboard abs, which used to give him a boxer's confidence that he could bounce back from any punch, were gone. Aches and inertia made Alain move like an old man in the days after the earthquake. He was wasting away and uninterested in doing anything about it, not even going home to Place Boyer. Instead, he lay awake on his cardboard for as long as he could until just the second before his new buddy, Philippe, the diminutive, cornrow-wearing leader of their refugee camp, who, it should be said, had turned out to be an even better leader in disaster relief than Alain was, came looking for him.

Alain was embarrassed by the brokenness of everything. The simple fact that Philippe did not look like he wanted to flee and find a corner in which to vomit at each sight, smell, and sound of their damaged compatriots in the refugee camp, as Alain did, kept convincing Alain that he was truly weak but should at least stick around to help. So he lay in his hot tent, wondering how he could die in a way that Xavier, Philippe, and their new dependents would forgive him for. He assumed no one suspected his posttraumatic stress disorder was leading him to contemplate suicide. He wrongly suspected that no one would care if he died. So many people had died in the quake and daily in the camp, how many tears could anyone muster for a cripple's parting, even if he was useful as the camp's resident translator? The problem was, life in the camp, ironically enough, made suicide fairly difficult. With Philippe softening aid workers with his soul brother–community leader act, Alain worked as a closer, hammering out arrangements with aid agencies to secure his little community precious necessities like food, water, hygiene kits, tents, his-and-hers toilets, separate men's and women's showers, and even lamps and lights to scare off potential rapists, thieves, and demons in the wee hours. Alain's ability to glad-hand and fake a condescending, look-at-these-poor-unlucky-Haitians, aren't-we-noble nod with the fey Canadian or haughty Frenchman or perky American in charge was offensive, but it translated into supplies for the families of Park Pigeon, so no one called him on it. The work still added to his depression, though. Under little Xavier's ever-present and ever-watchful eyes, Alain was careful to stay upbeat and solution-oriented. His compassion cup ran over—when in public. He had always been a good actor. Everyone, especially the foreign visitors, seemed too preoccupied and overwhelmed by Haiti—All that natural and stunning beauty! All those vacant, shocked faces! All those glistening bodies! The Middle Ages–level misery!—to scratch his smiley surface to see the morbidity that had spread over his soul like a cancer. These people never asked the obvious questions—You're from Place Boyer, what are you doing here? Place Boyer was unaffected by the earthquake, why don't you go home? Why are you still living in a tent? Isn't it dangerous here?—and Alain didn't have to figure out an answer.

Place Pigeon and the surrounding parks along the Champ de Mars teemed with thousands of earthquake refugees. They lived five or more people to a tent fit for two. They were cramped, tired, hurt, grieving for all the people and things, a world really, they had lost during the thirty-five-second earthquake. How can an event be so short and cause so much damage? People talked about that day, that quake, and their terror all the time. Oh, there were cries for help everywhere. All the survivors remembered hearing them as they made their way, or were made to make their way, out from under tons of rubble. But you had to ignore them, didn't you? Or you were made to ignore them by the sheer scale of your powerlessness, your infinite meekness? I can't believe we got to live.

My dear dead Natasha, Alain wrote, furtively, in the diary he began keeping in his tent.

Why did you leave me? I mean, *leave me* leave me. Oh I know why you left me, but where did the strength to

do so come from? I know I approved of the marriage. I
encouraged you to find a patron for your art. I needed
more time. You needed a nicer life ASAP. I got it. The
President's not a bad man. A weak man, a man without
a courageous bone in his body, but he was wise enough
to take the quasi-love you made available to him. You
gotta give him credit for that. We would have had great
stories to tell our children after you left him for me to
whom you rightfully belonged. Yeah, I said it. Belong.
I owned you like you owned me. I'm sorry.

I don't know what to do with my life now. I survived
the earthquake. I can't believe I survived the fucking
earthquake and you didn't. I'm supposed to be grateful.
It's some kind of miracle. I ain't grateful. You alive is the
miracle I would have preferred. The rest, I'm ashamed
to admit, is noise. Thousands of people like you are
dead. Estimates are wild. I've heard numbers as high
as 100,000! But nine million of us remain, no matter
what the number of earthquake deaths settle at. Probably half that number still living wishes they were dead
too; they persevere. I can't. You should see their tough-
ness at work. I'm not them. I can't handle life anymore.
My nerves are shot. My own shadow scares me. I refuse
to leave the refugee camp. I cannot bear the thought of
the world beyond it, my father, our house, our society,
and the flow of talk of books, politics, profits, children,
beaches, football, travel, America, reconstruction,
rubble, God. Maybe the earthquake shook away my

Haitianness, our supposed innate capacity to grin and bear all God's sick jokes. I don't know. I'm being useful in the country's darkest hour. I have a job, handling relations with foreigners who come around to offer help. I got our camp food, water, tents, first aids kits, even hygiene kits for girls, soccer balls, toilets, showers, even occasional police patrols. I have my own tent, lamp, pen, pad, cardboard to sleep on, crackers to eat, water. When it rained last night, I got mud too. I used it as a pillow. Might as well. My hair is falling out. The pillow was soft and gooey. Tasty too. Just kidding.

I have a roommate in my tent, just one roommate. A privilege. (Privilege, as you liked to point out, had a way of always finding me. It does even now in this damaged new world. At this rate, I'll probably have my own cabin in the Devil's cruise ship in hell.) Most people are piled in four to six in their tent. My roommate is a preternaturally mature orphan from nearby Fort National. He could be the Son of God, but I'm too afraid to ask. The last thing I want these days is to give my conflicted feelings about God a face to hate. I like the kid. He keeps me calm. You see, Natasha, I don't want to do anything with my life now that you're dead. I feel the country died too. Life as I knew it died that January afternoon. The new world is for the brave. I do not feel like one of them. Assuming you're in heaven—surely adulterers go to heaven—you have to tell me how to join you as quickly as possible. Send me a sign. You have to help me figure out a way to gracefully escape whatever is trying to pass as life here on earth after Ragnarok. It's gotten harder to kill yourself in Port-au-Prince since the quake, believe it or not. Or maybe mustering energy to do anything but lay in my tent—it is a nice tent; it's from Taiwan—and play-acting at public servant will wear out soon. Some invisible damage I suffered internally during the quake may end me. It's become a common phenomenon. We bury more seemingly unhurt people in the camp each day. It's like they decide to not wake up. We bury more of these people than we help mothers give birth! An old lady or man or child sits in a corner staring into space for days on end, looking stunned, just shocked, that the earthquake did what it did to them and then they either close their eyes and tumble from their seat onto the dirt or someone touches their unblinking face and discovers their souls had long fled their bodies.

Have you seen your mom in heaven? Does my grand-father walk with a limp up there too? Dad can't be dead, can he? Pétionville, I've heard, was spared by the quake. Shit, I should go check up on him. And mom too. If they're alive, they're probably worried sick about me. They approved of you, you know. I was only messing with you when I told you dad didn't like you. I suspect they liked you because they knew you wanted to leave here perma-nently and they wanted me to leave too. They worried too much about my safety. They should have worried about my heart breaking. I loved you so much.

In the thirty-sixth second, the earth stopped shaking, and a fog of dust fell like gentle snow on Port-au-Prince. On the ground of the airport's tarmac an old man in a torn suit lay flat on his back and performed snow angels in the dust with a big grin on his face. Of all the Haitian reactions to the earthquake, his will be the most scrutinized. His will be considered by millions of observers the world over as a call to arms or a call to surrender, or a reminder that death and life go on, and that life on earth was meant to suck, even when it seemed as though it could not suck worse than it did on the thirty-sixth second after the thirty-five-second tremor in Port-au-Prince that January afternoon. Slowly, oh so slowly, his eyes opened and took in . . . snowflakes? No, these flakes were small and dry. They caused the old man's eyes to itch and his grin, which was stupid but involuntary, to fade. The picture of grim determination, he rose on his elbows then to his feet, patting dust off his suit jacket as he went along. Near him a plane stood in an unflyable position. The airport's tower, as far as he could make out, had crumbled into itself, sending heaping chunks of red-and-cream concrete sprawling all the way to his tasseled loafers. The air smelled of brimstone. His throat felt choked. The first notes of the melody of his voice escaped him. However, a nauseating group of moaning voices belonging to others rose faintly, like mist, in the distance, the first sounds he'd heard since the sound of his voice got completely bossed by the mysterious force that ejected him off the airplane's steps. Above, the sun shone a hazy white light. Yet he felt cold. Am I dead? he thought. Before the old man could raise a hand to shield his eyes from the white sunlight, which had grown intense and was causing his head to throb, his vision blurred. He rubbed his eyes, hard, then a vision, dream, or nightmare appeared to him.

The scene was lit like the eye of a hurricane in a film, bright but surrounded by a cold darkness and winds that roared. A tall, bearded man stood behind a lectern. Behind the man the President saw the entrance to what looked like paradise: one of Haiti's idyllic beaches, like at Club Indigo, the kind of inheritance taken for granted by locals throughout the Caribbean but beloved by northern-dwellers. You never love something more than the moment you believe it to be lost. The President suddenly yearned to run and throw himself at full speed into the warm and blue sea that was his birthright. In front of him, however, was a line of about forty men, roughly the same size and age, but with different cuts of hair and clothes, reflecting different periods in Haitian history, from the Napoleonic era to the twenties to the bespectacled fifties to the guayabera-shirt eighties. The men were short and twitchy, and humbly looking at the ground or at the sky around them without saying a word.

A Napoleonic-costumed man was the first to meet Saint Peter. A hush fell over the group. The President started to recognize these guys. They were his predecessors. All of Haiti's dead presidents! He saw all the other presidents take a step back and work hard to pretend to ignore the conversation the guy in front was having with their maker. Saint Peter was in a foul mood.

Dessalines, is it? he said. Looking at your ledger here, I see some truly remarkable achievements. You were a general in an army that fought and won a great war to bring freedom to slaves. Slaves! Saint Peter looked at the tall, dark man with the kind face standing behind him. The man nodded his approval. There are few acts we care for more than the emancipation of slaves. Freedom to choose your fate is Our Father's greatest gift to man and woman. You did Him proud. Your countrymen had been slaves for centuries. Centuries! My word. The odds! The courage! Dignity is the highest and one of the greatest gifts you could give your fellow man.

But . . .

But?

Jean-Jacques Dessalines hesitated.

But what? Saint Peter intoned. The plaza got really warm.

But, Mr. Peter, I don't feel worthy of heaven.

With a weary look on his wizened face, Saint Peter said, And why is that, General Dessalines?

I killed too many people to feel worthy of heaven, sir. I even had women and children killed after we won the war. Rage and darkness won me over for too long, long after I think I should have let it go. I couldn't let it go. How could the Father forgive me? I lost my head and couldn't turn the other cheek.

Then Dessalines began to cry. His sobs echoed across all the way to the President at the back of the line.

Do you know how you died, General? Saint Peter asked.

I don't know, sir. Last thing I remember is that we were near Pont Larnage and there was an ambush. My cortege was surrounded. Lots of voices screamed confusing and contradictory orders at me. Stay inside! Come out! Show your face! Stay quiet! A bunch of arms broke inside and reached for me. Then the world went black. I don't know for how long. The first light I saw was the one that led me to your feet.

I'll say, Saint Peter said. It probably wasn't a good idea for you to name yourself emperor of Haiti a few years into your presidency. The people were still angry at the French emperor.

I know.

Emperor!

I know, I know.

That politically tone-deaf move made you a dead man walking thereafter. The last thing your people wanted so soon after overthrowing Napoleon was another emperor.

Sigh.

What your people need is someone in charge of a government, autocratic or not, who serves their needs, dignity, and children first. Any form of government that did just that would do. Do you want to know who had you killed?

No.

Really? It would be no trouble for us. We can introduce them to you right now. Your killers, by the way, hacked your body into multiple pieces. The woman who collected your dead body for a proper burial had to make multiple trips.

No, no, thank you. I don't want to meet my Judas.

Good answer. Now, would you please step aside for a minute while we hear your successor make his case for heaven? You look disappointed.

I thought you'd send me straight to hell.

Why, you're in a hurry! It's eternity. Hell, or heaven, for that matter, is not going anywhere. You and your people present us with a complicated case. We could use more time and evidence to deliberate before making our decision on your fates. Your inability to collectively band to develop that pretty island caused millions of people to needlessly suffer malnutrition and other cruel forms of death for generations. Sending people to hell when they had resources and know-how to save or improve millions, and in some cases, billions of lives on earth but failed to do so out of a smallness of spirit, a self-centered form of evil, is easy. You people, on the other hand, lived in hell already, the hell of slavery followed by a hellish poverty cocreated by your unforgiving former slave-masters. Your poor judgment still came down to vanity, an excessive amount of amour propre. Remember the first of the Ten Commandments, General Dessalines?

Er, no.

Of course you don't. It's "Thou shall not have other gods before me."

I believe you are mistaken, sir. I had no other God before God, Dessalines said. I bowed to no man!

Sure, you did, Saint Peter said, you worshipped yourself more than you worshipped God.

In the back of the long line of dead Haitian presidents, the last President swallowed hard. He watched his predecessors face Saint Peter one by one and come up wanting. Dessalines was followed by one of the men who may have had him killed, Henri Christophe, then Alexander Pétion, Jean Pierre Boyer, Charles Rivière-Hérard, Philippe Guerrier, Jean-Louis Pierrot, Jean Baptiste Riché, Faustin Soulouque, Fabre Geffrard, Nissage Saget, Sylvain Salnave, Michel Domingue, Pierre Boisrond-Canal, Joseph

Lamothe, Lysius Salomon, François Légitime, Monpoint Jeune, Florvil Hyppolite, Tirésias Simon Sam, Pierre Nord Alexis, François Antoine-Simon, Cincinnatus Leconte, Tancrède Auguste, Michel Oreste, Oreste Zamor, Joseph Davilmar Théodore, Vilbrun Guillaume Sam, Philippe Sudré Dartiguenave, Louis Borno, Louis Eugène Roy, Sténio Vincent, Élie Lescot, Franck Lavaud, Dumarsais Estimé, Paul Eugène Magloire, Joseph Nemours Pierre-Louis, Franck Sylvain, Léon Cantave, Daniel Fignolé, Antonio Kebreau. To a man, they told Saint Peter to send them to hell. They could have been better men, they said. Then, one step ahead of the President came the turn of the so-called devil himself, President Dr. François Duvalier.

The man standing in the shadow behind Saint Peter cleared his throat. Peter looked at the diminutive and be-spectacled dictator like an old acquaintance. Duvalier, he said. Let's look at your ledger, shall we?

The day got considerably warmer.

Really, Duvalier said, do we have to? My ledger's negatives are no different than those of any head of state to face this lectern in the history of man. I confess freely to physically and emotionally destroying my enemies and other irritants, both to win power and to stay in power during my long rule. My country had the reflexive dislike of authority more commonly found among teenagers. They needed a president with a strong hand. Right, fellas?

The dozens of ex-presidents sitting in stands in nearby purgatory did not answer.

I killed men and women with my own hands and the hands of my armed forces, he said. Did I get any further than my illustrious predecessors in figuring out a form of government to take care of the needs of our nation's citizens? No. I couldn't decide between capitalism and communism. I dithered and failed to come up with a third way. The power to turn sand and gravel into bread and lettuce to feed our masses never came to me despite my prayers. My citizens ended up the poorer for it, though not as poor as they became under the incompetent fools who took over trying to develop the place after my death.

With that, François Duvalier turned around and looked at the President with more than a bit of disgust. The President felt his cheeks heat up. So many narratives, so many stories, so many faiths he clung to, shattered that instant. So many people told him and the world that François Duvalier was the anti-Christ, the worst man and Haitian to have ever walked the earth. He had lived the Duvalier era and survived and even thrived. But he felt its craven impotence in his bones. He saw it in the faces of his parents and neighbors and the widows and orphans of Duvalier's murder sprees. The man bathed the country with negative energy. Even artists and poets felt their talents wilt at the thought of facing the idea of Duvalier. Only Natasha, his brilliant and precocious child bride, had the courage and wit to take on the *diable*. When he saw her canvas titled *Duvalierism*—a white canvas painted thickly and slickly black, a Rothko without a halo's glow—tears streamed down his face. He was speechless. And now here he was, listening to Duvalier himself make a credible case to Saint Peter for his access to heaven. I loved, Duvalier was saying. I loved my wife and did everything I could to sustain her love, to keep her approval, her pride, and her affection. We had only one boy, and I loved him like few other fathers loved their son. I loved him like He loved His son. Like Him, I bequeathed a kingdom to my son. Like His son, the great power and our world's great needs and flaws overwhelmed my son. *Peu importe*. I did my duty. I served my people as best I could. I fulfilled my duties as a loving father, husband, son, cousin, nephew, uncle, and citizen as best I could. I died in office in my bed, peacefully. Only six out of forty Haitian presidents can boast of such an accomplishment. I left my children a legacy of strength and wealth of resources that served them well for decades. Excuse my lack of modesty, Peter. It's an old man's habit. But I really do look forward to eternal life in heaven.

Peter's eyebrow shot up.

Oh? he said.

You've read my heart, Duvalier responded calmly. And you've read my press. Was the little patch of earth I was responsible for better off during my time there than after? It was, wasn't it?

Seemingly amused, Saint Peter asked, And what about the human rights you denied your citizens? The democracy you denied your country by staying in power for so long, and then passing governance over to your son as if it were a vintage watch? What about the highly preventable poverty you allowed your people to sink into? What say you, doctor?

Riveted by Duvalier, a Dante verse floated through the President's mind. It had the melody of a Smokey Robinson song.

> His face was the face of a just man,
> So mild, if you looked no deeper than the skin;
> The rest of his body was a reptile's . . .

Except in this vision, this glimpse of his future through the fates of his predecessors as they met their maker, the rest of the body of Duvalier that the President could see was that of a man, a small, stupid man.

On earth, Mr. Peter, the dictator said, the incentives weren't aligned right for me to do more than I did. I'm a simple man with simple tastes. I didn't travel much. I didn't want more from life than I had. I rarely ever left the palace, my home. I was a man caring for my family as best as I could, like all men try to care for their families. What did I care that the roads to Hinche or Jérémie were shit? What did I care that people couldn't vote, and the constitution was unreliable? Our education system was all right. They wanted to speak French. We gave them French. The people wanted to talk more than build. They wanted to study more than work. They wanted to pose more than serve. Talk, talk, talk, study, study, study. Dance, drink,

drink. Fuck. They got that. If they wanted more, if they wanted to serve the land that birthed and fed us, they would have worked, innovated, and developed it. They played the short game. They got the country they worked for. They had the ambitions of children, so we treated them like children. What are you going to do, send all of us Haitians to hell because we had the attention span and work ethic of an orgasm? You got to give me credit for never leaving. Not that they were doling out Mediterranean retirement plans back then.

Again, Duvalier paused to turn around and give a stern look to the President in the eyes. What, the President thought, you of all people find me wanting? If a chocolate-brown man could blush, the President's face would have turned red. There was a big-enough grain of truth in Duvalier's contempt for him that his pride felt cut in a place he didn't know existed. Before Duvalier could go on, Saint Peter raised a hand and stopped him. Thank you, Dr. Duvalier, he said with finality. We have heard enough. We shall render our verdict on your fate.

Now sweating as if his body were already halfway submerged in hellfire, the President watched the saint's face closely to gauge his reaction to Duvalier's plea. As the verdict became clearer and clearer, the President suddenly saw another grand, glorious nimbus of light. The fierce fire looked as if heaven itself had opened up to swallow or eradicate them all. Afraid, the President turned away.

Opening his eyes, he discovered that he had returned

to Toussaint Louverture Airport's tarmac. Ruined, broken Toussaint Louverture Airport in the wan afternoon sun was a happy sight for his sore eyes. The President felt relieved, light-headed, and, for the first time in a life steeped in passive-aggression, determined. He felt as if he had received from God a reprieve from an almost guaranteed trip to hell. His own date with Saint Peter had been delayed. He didn't know how much time he had left. From what he saw up there—or was it down there?—anything can happen after you die. There might be an opportunity for him to get certain things right, or to right certain things he believed he may have gotten wrong, royally wrong, all his life. Where to start?

Mr. President! Mr. President!

They were soldiers, young and unhurt. Foreign. They stood at attention with spines straight, cream-colored jaws squared. They awaited orders. His. His hearing was off, way off. Dust caked his lips as though he had been eating sand all afternoon. There was work to do.

Mr. President, come with us.

Excuse me?

Sir.

What?

Sir!

That's better. Talk to me.

A Captain Waughray, a dark-eyed London cop turned blue-helmeted United Nations neocolonialist masquerading as a peacekeeper, told the President the sad tale of the earthquake that had risen unexpectedly from a shift of tectonic plates deep beneath the Caribbean Sea to destroy Port-au-Prince as he knew it forever. The President took in the news soberly. He began to search for the right and bright new words to soothe his people in this, their darkest hour since they had been French slaves. He blocked out the impulse to acknowledge the freakiest fact, that in his sixty years never once had anyone he knew or anything he'd read about in his lifelong study of Haitian history mentioned the word "earthquake" as a part of life on the island. In his role as a natural then popular elected leader of the community, tragedy had been his daily bread. When people read the common description of Haiti as the poorest country in the Western Hemisphere, he often thought that they probably had no clue what living that fact was like for a sensitive person. Though his heart had filled with doubt about the quality and number of virtues Saint Peter, Jesus, and God would find in there, he knew his capacity to absorb and help others cope with the torrential pour of unexpected bad news that often characterized life in Haiti was true. So he walked briskly toward a hastily built command center on the tarmac surrounded by a half-dozen earnest and strong young men, and he hurried his emotions to process and discard as quickly as possible the potential pain the disaster may have caused him personally. His wife, his mother, his relatives, friends, and protégé were out there, caught in the brief but deadly maelstrom, and they were unaccounted for so far. *Les soldats étrangers s'en foutent.* So should he, for now, he decided.

Sitting down felt nice, even on a metal chair. The tent was meant to be his own. The foreign soldiers handed him a bottle of Evian, a sandwich, and a wet towel so he could wipe his face and attempt to freshen up. They apologized for the lack of air conditioning. It should be operational in the morning, they said. The President chased away a bitter thought about how these Americans—and all foreigners in Haiti, to him, were either American or largely funded by America, which made them, often, even more American—could have all these creature comforts and resources so at the ready, so nearby, that they could mobilize them so quickly after such a disaster. The air conditioning in my office at the National Palace hasn't worked in a year, but I'll have an air-conditioned tent in the middle of an airport runway within twenty-four hours of the nation's destruction. The irony. The American armed forces had sent a slew of giant airplanes. His gracious hosts were beginning an informal occupation, a tightening of a grip meant to keep his country stable, which was a far cry from healthy, and a galaxy away from developed or even developing. This state of affairs is to be a source of strength for you, old man. A state of grace. The Americans blanketed the darkening sky with jumbo jets, dropping off men and supplies whose silent footfall reminded the President of midday summer rains in Jacmel or November snowfalls in Montreal. The President listened to the hum of activity surrounding his tent for a while, then dozed off in his metal chair. The cool of the Port-au-Prince night greeted him when he woke up, fitfully, to the sight of Captain Waughray, poker-faced but youthful, almost kind.

Sir, we have a situation, he said.

His wife held him. They held each other. He wept. Natasha's grip was strong; her fingers dug holes in his skin. He bled, happily. Her relief came in shuddering waves of emotion. This must be how a child would hold her father after a near-death experience, he thought. Such transporting, intense love was something he could only imagine, because he had never had children, which was very unusual for a man of his age and standing in Port-au-Prince. It was a lapse that would haunt him to his grave.

The next day, he woke up to life in a tent in a ruined city at a loss for words. He busied himself mastering the art of nodding sagely to United Nations and/or American military officers during their briefings on the health, education, infrastructure, economic, and political effects of the earthquake. The briefings were constant. The data dizzying. The range of trauma stupefying. The death toll caused by the earthquake grew exponentially seemingly by the minute. He began to feel as though the earth had kept on shaking and killing more of his people all day long after its splashy thirty-five-second eruption. His mind found it harder and harder to accept the fact that such a brief tremor could cause such carnage. The whole world is with Haiti, the foreigners told him. The outpouring of aid is unprecedented. You are not alone. That's how the officers concluded each briefing. For some reason, each time he heard the pat phrases he cringed. This is between us and God, he wanted to say. We appreciate your help. Could you please leave our island now? Instead, he nodded.

Natasha spent the day sleeping, or lying in her cot in their tent with her back turned away from him and the world. Her mind was far away and seemingly unreachable to him. He was afraid of what she was thinking. Did she also think me unworthy? Could she validate me?

That night, when the emergency camp at the airport was asleep, and even the millions of newly homeless Haitians around the city slept to keep from weeping, he suffered great anxiety. The cure wasn't going to be found on the island. He scurried behind a pile of rubble, sat down, fished out his cell phone, and dialed a number he hadn't dialed in years but remembered by heart. The phone rang an unfamiliar tone. What time was it in South Africa? Only an hour later than Paris. He should be awake.

Bernard Métélus speaking.

Hello?

Hello?

The President cleared his throat. Forgive me, Father, I have sinned, he said. It's been six years since my last confession.

Seated in a car in the parking lot of the University of Johannesburg's Soweto campus, Father Métélus, a defrocked priest and former president of Haiti, turned off the engine and covered his mouth to suppress a gasp. His oldest friend in the world was on the phone. In the twenty four hours since the earthquake had struck down Haiti, he had been famished for news from home. After a sleepless night watching CNN, Bernard Métélus had decided he had a good-enough feel for the scale of the tragedy to stop listening to foreigners' takes on it, either on TV or in the faculty lounge at the university. He did have a good laugh when a Rwandan criminology professor told him he felt sorry for Haiti and added, It was a shame to see so many people naked and barefoot and desperate on TV like that. Why can't they get it together? Easy, buddy, Métélus wanted to say, Haiti has its failings, but we never up and killed a million of our own in one month, like your people did in the nineties. But Métélus had long ago become accustomed to the absurdly extreme reactions Haiti provoked in people around the world. So he bit his tongue and spent his time swimming in nostalgia of his favorite places in Port-au-Prince: La Saline, Cité Soleil, Champ de Mars, Paco, Carrefour Feuilles. He liked that his heart had seemed to accept the probable premature deaths suffered by many of his loved ones with a certain amount of Zen. Maybe his old priestly wisdom hadn't completely disappeared after all. He now realized that his calm in the face of his wife's and other Haitians' hysterical reactions to the horrific event back home was a front. The sound of the voice of an old friend, even one who had become a colleague he despised and a successor he dismissed, pierced a thick wound he long thought healed. His emotions outran him, spilling tears through his eyes and spectacles, sandpapering his throat. If the President had survived the gruesome destruction of the National Palace, maybe Tante Evelyne in Léogâne survived too? Maybe my domino-player buddies in Carrefour survived too? Maybe the daughter in Port-au-Prince whose existence I had to deny survived also? Maybe the Lord does finally have mercy on me? Maybe He forgives my hubris? Maybe, just maybe, He loves me still. Maybe, just maybe . . . and then Bernard Métélus, failed Roman Catholic priest and politician in exile, for the first time in a long, long time, felt hope fill his soul, like fresh air through the lungs of a drowned man left for dead.

Go on, my son, Métélus said, with a quivering voice.

PART II

—

Now it is time that we were going, I to die and you to live; but which of us has the happier prospect is unknown to anyone but God.

—Socrates, in Plato's *Apology*

THE PRAYER

Five minutes before the earthquake no one knew was coming destroyed everything everyone held dear, Natasha Robert was a confused young newlywed, standing on the tarmac of Toussaint Louverture Airport in Port-au-Prince. She was clutching a one-way ticket out of Haiti, worried she had married the wrong man and wondering whether God would forgive her for that sin. I love you, she whispered to the memory of the other man, her ex-lover. But I cannot be with you anymore. I must leave Haiti. Please leave me be, she said to herself with mounting anxiety. Grant me peace! Please? The memory took the shape of a stone-faced ghost, and the ghost showed her no pity. The young woman was the only person in the presidential entourage assembled at the airport who saw the ghost, so no one outside her head could hear her scream. The air smelled a woozy mix of Caribbean sea and jet engine fuel. Primly dressed in a formal white-

and-black dress, and standing on a tarmac that glittered, positively glittered, under a bright sun, Natasha tried to blink away her past in favor of a swanky future. The effort stalled. One last memory lingered. The memory was a good one too, seemingly endless and sweet. The winter day had been unusually hot. To all the world, Natasha looked the picture of poised, exquisite, and carefree beauty. But her heart nursed a wound inflicted by her head, and now it was fit to burst if she didn't get herself together. Tears were on the verge of ruining her makeup. A disaster of epic proportions. She should be happy. She was about to have one of her childhood dreams come true—Leaving Haiti for good! Yay!—but the image of a handsome young man, a dreamboat with a nightmare's poor timing, came jarringly into her mind, wrecking her nerves, breaching the dam of her cool facade. Why am I seeing your ghost when I know you to be alive and well? she thought. Feelings for this man, her heart insisted on reminding her, the young man she'd jettisoned recently for a wealthier and much older man, and, in the process, casually, cruelly, and pretty much completely breaking both their hearts, surfaced in her chest with a vehemence that stopped her in her tracks. She stood still in the middle of the group. The group was in a hurry. The airplane they were about to take for a permanent leave of their island nation shimmered like a mirage under the assault of the Caribbean heat. The plane, like most escape fantasies, looked as though it could disappear before they reached it.

This made folks nervous. Their nerves weren't helped by the fact that the tarmac's asphalt was so hot it was melting the soles of their loafers and high heels. Some began to fear for the fate of the bottom of their feet. Their feet could not possibly put up a better fight than Italian leather did. As if alone, or, to her impressionable new friends, on a movie set, Natasha loosened her collar, lost in her thoughts, still not walking toward her husband, who was at the head of the queue, a hand imperiously thrust at her.

Until the moment she abruptly stopped the exodus, Natasha had been all smiles; an award-winning, movie-star-worthy grin, her entourage noted early and often. Her smile was indeed winning. All her life, its brilliance seduced women and men, boys and girls, soldiers and nuns, and elders and babies. Recently, her gentle yet arresting beauty had ensnared a head of state and his entourage and her nation, too—well, the small percentage of the population with access to television sets. Her wedding day was like a national holiday. Their every move became an opportunity to celebrate rare national glamour. Even on this treacherous day, when the first couple secretly planned to ditch Haiti for Italy, smatterings of cheering throngs accompanied their procession from the National Palace to the national airport for what the President's public relations people billed as the new first couple's first foreign tour, featuring a first stop in Florence, Italy, to support Haitian artists featured at a biennale in the Uffizi. To be fair, crowds lined the streets of Port-au-Prince all the time.

Sidewalks were too narrow or nonexistent throughout the city. The streets contained more adults, children, dogs, pigs, sometimes cats, bikes, puddles, and garbage piles at all hours than the overcrowded and lightly governed city could handle. Still, in a disturbingly short amount of time, Natasha had grown attached to the cheers, the approval of strangers. They had the livening effect of a good new drug. The first pangs of withdrawal pain already loomed in her spirit's outer edges. On good days, or during good moments on uneven days, the flush of mass approval justified Natasha's choice of husband and nursed her shattered and shamed heart. Life was golden, her entourage told her. You're so beautiful, they said. You're so lucky.

Damn right, she thought.

Natasha was only two days removed from a walk down the aisle with the most eligible bachelor in town, the president of the republic. Since their first date at the opening of the Orphan Art Gallery in Carrefour, he'd repeatedly told her that for the rest of his natural life his business would be the business of securing her health, wealth, and happiness. To love her to death. Everyone told Natasha that the President went to great lengths to impress her, shocking lengths in fact. Even now, during her ill-timed fit of buyer's remorse, her husband was too busy being good to her to notice. He was multitasking, executing a slight of hand that would soon allow them to escape his duties to Haiti and hand her a posh life in Tuscany. On the other end of his cell phone was his longtime right-hand man, Reginald Leglise. Reginald was a source of good humor and as reliable as the sunrise. The President had charged him with securing the final details from US Embassy officials on everything from the President's retirement cash flow in his Swiss bank accounts to hotel reservations to the day's flight schedule. Port-au-Prince to Florence. Nonstop. Sweet.

Stay on them, the President said. Don't let them out of your sight until you hear from me and I tell you we landed safely in Italy. All that is mine here will then be yours, old friend, as promised. No, not the National Palace. Very funny, Reginald. Thanks, I needed that. You're right. I have been through a lot in recent weeks. This deal took a lot out of me. It's a beauty though, isn't it? My best ever. What can I say? It's not like we had a pension system here to take care of me after my last term ended. Our people hate to pay taxes. They miss out on so much, the poor fools.

Natasha generally admired her husband's ability to make people feel sorry for him when they shouldn't. Not today. Today, the absence of scruples in his charm made her feel ordinary, small. A silver-tongued coward's plaything. Marie Antoinette with a melanin overdose. Natasha never felt ordinary with . . . she still dared not speak her ex-lover's name. His smirking ghost stood by her side, staring. Seeping courage from her. Natasha felt her grip on the world crumple in shades of bright green and yellow like a cubist painting. If . . . he . . . was unmuted,

Natasha knew, her ex-lover would tell her the old man was unworthy of her, that he was a lousy president who had barely scratched the surface of possibilities of carrying out his great responsibilities as leader and protector of the dignity of their people, even in tasks as easy as rebuilding an airport with American Airlines' money. He'd describe to Natasha the myriad ways the airport could and should have been better than it had been. And she would see the possibilities for transformation and improvement come alive in her mind's eye. Then she'd reach for a sketch pad and start drawing images, a story that would come to her first as a low tickle in the bottom of her heart and then as a burst of rainbow-colored flavors in her creative id that she would need to tamp down over days to create a memorable and pleasant painting or sculpture. She was never too sure if these bursts of brain-frying inspiration happened because of the power of his words and ideas or the curves of his lips and the sparkle of his confident dark-brown eyes when he talked and touched her, or touched her while talking to her. He always touched her whenever she was near, lightly, sharply, sometimes pointedly, always possessively, intensively, and suggestively. His whole body spoke to hers whenever possible. Tickling bursts of excitement would fill her with each contact, almost literally lighting her up. When they went on walks during escapes to Wahoo Bay Beach. When they had dinner in his house on Place Boyer or in her room at the National Palace. (He often ate *fritaille*, a local mixture of spicy fried pork or goat chunks, plantains, and turkey, brought from the streets; she often ate a three-course meal prepared by the President's ageless and spice-loving chef.) In a voice that seemed incapable of a yellow note of doubt, he often described in thrilling detail how the surrounding architecture, traffic, economy, foreign policy, art and music, constitution, infrastructure, agriculture, one arcane law after another, could be improved, tweaked, just so to make all Haitians' lives better. Socialism mixed with a correct dose of capitalism ain't that hard, he'd say. We just have to get over our commitment issues first. That boy had no sense of jobs and process and politics. But, man, could he talk up dreams.

Lost in her thoughts, Natasha hadn't realized she had been moving forward, gliding toward the plane against her will. The President's entourage subtly pushed her from behind, as they were wont to do, toward her husband, who was still talking on the phone but waiting for her. The white heat and the noise of the revving jet engines licked her face. The black droning sound and the smell of the exhaust pummeled her. The combination made Natasha dizzy. The moment, this dream-concretizing climax, felt ephemeral. Like she was about to wake up where she was born, in a roofless orphanage, naked, afraid, hungry, but pugnacious.

Really, why does the memory of the most painful moment of my life go together with my love for that guy? Really, God, what's that all about? Is that more proof that

I need to get away from him and his country as quickly and as far away as possible? The beginning thump of a throbbing headache emerged. Natasha thought of the unsolvable paradox of love and regrets. Love did have its upsides, she conceded. The feeling triggered a swelling and crashing of warm waves of emotions inside her. The waves grew stronger, especially now that the old man who was now her old man, a husband she liked but did not love, was living up to his promise to sweep her off their godforsaken island, inspiring her to inch closer to loving him, or at least to the point where she began experiencing glimmers of love's cousins—affection, tenderness, awe, faith—toward him, but not quite love, for she was naturally frugal with her love, nipping it in the bud early and often in her young life except once. It's not like she had much choice. The young man's presence in her life seemed to ignite her life, as if she didn't exist without his attention. The connection felt normal and permanent and urgent. Permanently urgent. But it doesn't have to be a relationship, the chorus of prostitutes who lived near the orphanage had told her. These girls told her to remember that she was unusually pretty and charming and quick. It was her duty to use those God-given gifts to marry up, for richer and older wealth and security, and this young man, smart as he was, dashing as his military-perfect posture made him seem to be, and wealthy and honest as his square and steady gaze promised he could become, was no more richer than us whores today, and not worth too much of her time. He could be your lover, they said, *ton petit ami*, but never anything more, not even her boyfriend, and that would be OK. Her meager origins made it so. Haiti's hardships ratified it. Provided you were tough enough to walk away from him for good within a minute of landing a rich man, you could play around with him, they said. That's what these attractive girls expected from their future and demanded Natasha expect from hers. The mythical rich man who erases all deprivations. The girls were mostly newbies in a self-defeating game, but they were diligent about what passes for its learned wisdom. They alternated between recruiting Natasha and advising her to be smarter than they were about love, sex, and men. Natasha took their sisterly advice with a grain of salt. Today, while wallowing in guilt in the glow of her lottery ticket of a husband, she realized how closely she had actually followed the whores' script. She remembered, also, that her new old man was human too and also haunted by his childhood's deprivations. At this delicate hour of his life, Natasha would do well to behave like a supportive wife. She scolded herself to get it together.

Natasha's parents, for the brief years she knew them, were big on confessions. They weren't the first parents in their neighborhood to give their adorable five-year-old daughter away to an orphanage in hopes she'd get to eat at least one meal a day, but they may have been the first parents to not promise they'd come back for said daughter after they got back on their feet. In their small apartment in the Fort National neighborhood of Port-au-Prince, her mother often told her that nothing good ever came to beggars whenever Natasha begged her parents for things, like food or water, or a toy to play with. Her mom, who'd given birth to her only child in the same orphanage she had been born in about sixteen years earlier, said no. No. Every. Single. Time. Her mother was an authority on begging, for she was a beggar, *une professionelle*. So there was no point in begging God, Maman scolded. Few men and women in the history of the world had begged God for mercy and better fortunes than her good, Catholic people had for the last five centuries. Look what that's gotten you? If you want something, her mother said, you better not even whisper it to your so-called God, not if you really want it. You think I'm bad, but no one says no more consistently than Him.

Compared to my mother at my age, my present situation was not that bad, Natasha thought. The tarmac, the achingly blue sky, the private jet, the blue-helmeted soldiers, the sweltering heat, her wide-backed, soft-chinned husband, the look of envy in the eyes of the men who were his staff and friends, and the chirpiness of their other halves—but the torment of guilt would not disappear. Jesus, all that Catholic schooling, all those Masses, all that Bible reading and gospel singing, all those paintings, and only now, as I am about to betray my one true love, as I am about to prove my ignorance of the meaning of love, of You, my Lord, only now do I finally get it. I was supposed to love him for love's sake.

Am I losing my mind as punishment? And you, the silent ghost, what are you looking at? Could you please tell me what to do, you mute fool? My parents would have something useful to say during this crisis. But they've been gone awhile now, haven't they, God? Since you took them from me for no good reason, how about imparting a girl with some wisdom in this crossroad?

You know what, maybe I'm already sorted. I may actually love this fat old man. Maybe the feeling is so strange and novel and awesome, and its capacity to make me feel drunk, selfish, and even self-mutilating is so intense that I dare not say the name of the emotion even to myself, for surely love could bloom from the gratitude I feel towards him. Yes, love could. It could spring from such a well, slowly but worthily, unlike *coups de foudre* and the black rages they alternate and die with. Yes, love could. Unless hate came first.

Natasha? her husband said, snapping his fingers and nudging the girl out of her agita. The ghost of her great love blinked out of existence.

The President held his hand out to her. Natasha's new husband had the unwelcome habit of asking her to hold his hand whenever he wanted to reassure himself of something or whenever he felt her attention slipping away from him, like a father to a child. Like a child, she hated this request. She hated it when boyfriends her age did it. Today a lover forty years her senior was doing it. Sure, he had put a ring on it, but come on. His fingers were big, brown, and hairy, like a bear's, but with white hairs. Natasha couldn't help but throw up a little in her mouth.

Come, he said, poorly feigning patience.

With that simple word, the young girl lashed out at her husband, though she stood still on the tarmac with her mouth closed. Only her unblinking, unsmiling eyes, big, brown, and catlike conveyed her indignation. Was that an order? Who does he think he is? She felt the hairs on the back of her neck rise. I can't believe he did that, right here, right now.

The couple was walking toward a gleaming private jet for a one-way flight to Florence, Tuscany, Italy, in other words, heaven on earth; that is, if, like Natasha, you are a painter with fantasies of becoming an all-time great Catholic artist, like Da Vinci, Michelangelo, and Dante, even though Dante was a writer and not a painter. Natasha had loved Dante and all things Florentine since she'd stolen and read front to back and back to front a beat-up copy of Dante's *Divine Comedy* in Monsignor Dorélien's library when she was kid. Heaven and Florence, Dante's hometown, were Dante's obsessions. They slowly became Natasha's too, in no particular order. The irony that the *Divine Comedy* was a long poem about acute homesickness by a man who hated life in exile, and here she was, hoping for happiness in exile, was lost on her. The whole point of her marriage was to give her the freedom to fly off the island to live a life of adventure of her own choosing and not of fate's.

A memory of a recent night with her husband wafted before her eyes. So bold and proud in public, he was meek and anxious sexually, more often doomed than not. She looked at her husband with a flash of charitable eyes. Yes, he still had that damn hand thrust at her without even bothering to get off his stupid cell phone. Maybe he sensed her communion with the ghost of the young man he'd stolen her from. His professionally honed ability to read people frightened her. It sometimes seemed as though he could read minds. Still, he was about to give her Tuscany. That should buy him some consideration. He was old, so he should be allowed to be old-school. His manners, like the suede loafers he favored, were dainty and chivalrous. Where the young girl had seen imperiousness, a dash of guilt from her emotional betrayal of him made her see charm even though the white shirt, light blue suit, and purple pocket square he wore were jet-setish and goofy. Oh, the international headlines the next morning were going to be cruel.

Mr. President? she said. Did I do something wrong?

Come now, sweetheart, he said. That's no way to talk to your husband. How many times have I told you to call me Jean? You have that right now, you know. You are my wife. You are no longer the girl working in that awful orphanage. I'm no longer the president of Haiti. As of this morning I gave up the job, remember? I threw it all away for you, my love. In fact, once we get on that plane, I'll have the UN PR guy send a press release out telling the whole world that I shall be known henceforth as Mr. Natasha Robert. Your name will be my name. That's my new name. Do you like it? I like it. I think it has a nice ring to it.

Natasha did like it. She looked past his smiling eyes at the range of treeless brown mountains that bordered the airport. Two days earlier, they had gotten married in a hastily arranged ceremony that fell somewhere between a shotgun and a bazooka wedding. Held in Sacré Coeur, a small yet beautiful church, the ceremony struggled for cheer. The sky was overcast. The mood inside the church was rushed and tense. Sweat ran down her back, causing her body-fitting dress to cling too tightly to her muscular frame. They exchanged their vows in whispers at an altar filled with flowers and candles the scent of vanilla. The groom cried. The bride didn't. His ancient mother and seemingly even more ancient friends wore looks of disbelief. Many of them were giddy as girlfriends. Natasha suspected some of them had cashed in longtime bets on whether their buddy would ever make it down the aisle. She didn't invite anyone she knew to bear witness to their union. She didn't even tell her few friends about her wedding plans. They would have disapproved. Weren't you supposed to marry the other guy? they'd say, a reminder she didn't need. She wished to be as alone as possible during the transaction, er, event. She also hoped the event went by quickly, which it did; thus only now did Natasha Robert find herself asking questions with answers the young girl should have intuited much sooner, if she was into such things like forethought when it came to men.

Again, she thought of her parents. Such sweet losers. Her mother was a beggar, a peddler, and an all-around hustler. Her dear papa never had a job that she could think of, but somehow he rarely came home empty-handed. He could read too. Bedtime stories were the best. They had one book—*The Adventures of Pippi Longstocking* by Astrid Lindgren—but the best part of the night was after he'd close the book and talk to her. He told her she was the embodiment of his happiness, thus she was destined to always be happy. He told her this every night.

We were so happy you were born, he said. You were such a happy baby. We didn't have much, but we had love. We loved each other, and we loved you. *À mort*. We were badass about love.

The word "ass" made her laugh. It brightened her mood. We were badass about love. You used a bad word, Papa, she'd giggle, and voilà, all funk was lifted, the memory of her latest fight with her mother was swept under her spiritual rug.

Do you understand how much we love you, *chérie*?

Yes, Papa.

Never forget it, sweetheart, but, uh, don't use that language around your mom, OK? I don't want her to kick my ass. You know how she is. I ain't as tough as you are.

Oh, Papa, she'd swoon.

Papa wore an Afro and a handlebar mustache long after

they stopped being cool. Why don't men wear mustaches anymore? Papa came from the north, probably Port-de-Paix. He never specified. I was born in a manger deep in a jungle, he said. My parents were kind and God-fearing, so angels visited them after my birth, like they visited us after you arrived.

That was all he offered by way of origin story. It confused Natasha, but she was often too tired and grateful for his undivided attention to question it, choosing instead to listen quietly to the soothing purr of his baritone voice and romantic take on everything. At a young age, he said another night, I came to Port-au-Prince, alone, barefoot, and shirtless. My pants were too small. I was young, but I was happy to be here. This is the city of dreams. I was eager to get my piece of it. I was famished, you see. Hungry. My father had been a captain in the army back when we had an army. Our country had no obvious need for an army, but an army had freed us from slavery, and we grew paranoid about going back to slavery, so a new army had to be available to try to keep potential new slave-masters at bay. Anyway, a new president came into power at the peak of my father's powers and was kindly told by the foreigners who bankrolled his existence to disband the army, and disband it he did. Our family fell on hard times. Of course, our hardest times were nothing compared to the hard times of most of our neighbors. But still. Yes, dear, my father was an ex-mighty man. Nothing worse than a man of highly visible importance to his community fallen to the level of the ordinary. Papi struggled terribly with anonymity. That's partly why I hope you never develop a taste for alcohol or celebrity or both. Your grandfather had his flaws but he was a good man. He never cut a corner nor smiled unnecessarily. See these muscles on my arms? His were bigger. If he was a little bit corrupt, if he was one of those people who thought the job in the army was a crown and not a difficult public service for a difficult public in need of more services than the government had means to deliver, if he didn't worry about how I would think of him after word got out that he worked for the bad guys doing bad things, even though I was a child who thought he could do no wrong, if his legacy to me was less of a preeminent concern of his, which indirectly led to his loss of career and subsequent bankruptcy and love affair with Rhum Barbancourt—how that man, come to think of it, managed to drink himself to death, discreetly too, in our little *quartier*, is pretty fucking genius, *pardonne mon français*—if he was less noble, we'd be richer but much poorer for it. Because of his sense of honor we were never that poor.

Natasha laughed a small laugh. These confessions by her father often took place in her small candlelit room after her father had tucked her in bed, a bed made of cardboard and a too-small towel. He spoke carefully in a valedictory tone. It was as if he wasn't sure he'd be around or alive in the morning and he had to make sure Natasha knew the Robert family history. Like most things in their country, their familial existence was fragile and easily snuffed out by unexpected forces, he felt. If he didn't share their story with her, there was nowhere else for her to look it up. It wasn't recorded much anywhere else and whatever records did exist could disappear in a flash of random fires and other disasters, though her father often made clear that she had no reason ever to feel unlucky or cursed or any such nonsense.

Oh, Papa, she said. This was the way the sleepy little girl indicated she'd gotten her father's lesson *de la soirée* and wished to sleep. But Papa wanted her to like him and think him an honorable man. That these things mattered, that integrity and a sense of charity even when inhabiting a "borrowed" house with no roof in a country where any half-wit with a good smile could scare up money to live beyond his means, these were essential aspects of the Robert family character. He wanted five-year-old Natasha, and fifteen-year-old Natasha, and, hopefully, twenty-, thirty-, and fifty-year-old Natasha to remember these values as deeply and permanently as her pigmentation. Neither Papa nor young Natasha had any idea that Natasha would eventually become a twenty-year-old who'd sold her soul for a pot of gold.

She looked around her: a dozen stone-faced, armed, and oddly young Asian, Latino, and African soldiers stood behind her, the most powerful man in the country was in front, a jet with its engines running was impatiently welcoming her, open-ribbed. That morning, she had locked the one person capable of persuading her not to leave

Haiti in a bedroom closet. For good measure, she had thrown away the key. Yes, Natasha, she told her herself, you screwed up. There's no way out of this one. There won't be a do-over.

You know, Natasha, Ernst Robert, her papi, would say at the end of her bedtime sermon in a bid to keep Natasha's eyes from completely glazing over, You know, I know that all my talk about love, of legacies, honor, and family values will no longer be fashionable by the time you grow up and have to make tough decisions. They were already out of fashion when I was your age.

Fashionable or not, Papi said, being good for goodness' sake, and not simply for beneficial outcomes, is what separates us from the animals, sweetheart.

Damn it, Natasha, stop thinking about that boy, or else you're going to start crying again. A woman without grace—Papa'd say "woman" pointedly, like, this is no literary trick, I'm talking about you, girl; the candlelight at her bedside would flicker—a woman without grace and a sense of love towards her family will make decisions that could cause her enough grief to wound and scar and torture her for the rest of her life, a living death of a life, let me tell you. You betray your soul and you never get to live it down. Trust me. I know. There are worse ways to kill yourself than drinking yourself to death. Just look down your street. Just look at some of the faces on the sidewalk, on porches, hell, the stories on the radio, all the begging, all the false pride, there are way worse ways . . .

Papa would then shake his head in sadness for broken families and wayward children turned wayward adults. As a little girl listening to these sermons, Natasha had only a faint idea of what her father was talking about. The girl dug the moments just the same. She felt loved by his undivided attention. The care and tenderness were heavy and sweet. That's all that mattered to her. Her father's brown eyes got smoky. Come with me, he said, come forgive your mother for loving you too hard, you lovable brat.

Papa would get up, turn and walk, and expect me to follow him like I was his equal, his friend. He'd never ask for my hand, like I was too mature for that. I'd grab his hand with both of mine anyway and nuzzle against his strong arm. He'd soften up his posture. I held on to him with both hands way longer than I needed and way tighter than I would hold on to anything else ever in my life.

Natasha stared at her new husband's hand with a fine layer of horror. On his ring finger he wore a big gold ring crowned with blue diamonds. The diamonds sparkled in the afternoon sun. She felt the full weight of the cliché she was becoming collapse on her shoulders after months of denial. The cliché her ex who shouldn't be an ex probably believed she had become, and, worse, probably always thought she would become. Part of her hated the ex for being right. And she loved him, too, despite her desperate wish to stop doing so. If she ever saw him again—and the feelings this thought created gave her heartburn—if he forgave her for what she did to him, the ordeal her rejection put him through, if she saw him again, just one more time, even if it was only to say a proper good-bye, she would be straight with him. She would love him for who he was and no longer hold all the things he wasn't against him. On that day, she, the poor girl made damn good, would hope she would be spared the look of disappointment her father in the real heaven would someday give her if they ever met. She knew winning her ex-lover's forgiveness would require her to withstand her lover's pain. The boy would make her feel like shit. Or worse, he would go all Haitian on her and fucking hide his disappointment from her rejection with a shrug and a blank, distant, higher-minder stare. Indifference. Oh, that would kill her. She would rather die now than experience the killing stroke of his indifference.

Is something the matter, Natasha? the President said, his face obscured by the shadow cast by the immense erect American Learjet.

No, Natasha said. Everything's fine. *Allons, chérie.* With that, Natasha clasped her husband's hand fully. She squeezed the hand too, for good measure. The President was so visibly relieved his face and body shrank. He closed his cell phone and began climbing the stairs to get on the airplane with Natasha in tow. However, the minute Natasha put her foot on the first step, the earth shook. Wildly, like a beast. Then came the roar of an explosion, like the cracking of the biggest oak tree ever—the tree of life?—

and the ground split and splintered, into ever-growing waves that extended as far as the eye could see. As if she weighed as little as a doll, the force picked Natasha up and threw her backward, but the ground reached her before she could begin a downward arc. The ground rose up to hit her, repeatedly, and rapidly, so quickly, in fact, she barely felt the blows. The sound beneath the wave of earth reaching for her was a roar, a guttural outburst like the explosion of thousands of volcanoes. The roar horrified and enveloped Natasha. It suffocated her, and she found herself floating, body-surfing in a cocoon of violent sounds. Her arms and fingers flailed, clutching nothing but air. In her panic, she looked to the soldiers for help. They were too busy being crushed by tons of cream-painted walls. The airport's walls casually snuffed out their lives and newly lit cigarettes, as the falling walls of nearly every building in Port-au-Prince did to almost everyone else in their way that instant.

Alain! Natasha screamed, with, presumably, her dying breath.

A CLOSET IN THE NATIONAL PALACE

The morning before the earthquake struck, Alain Destiné was trapped in a closet in the National Palace, paralyzed with self-pity after losing his girlfriend. Sitting on a carpeted floor, naked as a bird and staring at his shriveled glory with a dumbfound look, he spent the entire day trying to figure out how his luck had run out on him. How he didn't get the girl. Before getting trapped in the closet, he was splayed on Natasha's large bed in a sea of creamy silk sheets, awash in a postcoital glow. Caressed by streams of pale yellow light filtering through the venetian blinds of his lover's mansion in the center of town, Alain watched the love of his life pack her things to leave him and their country for another man, yet, out of habit, for he was a born optimist, he still liked his chances of changing her mind.

Last night was incredible, baby, he said. He joked that she shouldn't put their condoms away too early.

I'm almost ready for round four.

Alain did that, joke when life was taking a bad turn. Natasha wore that studious look she got whenever she wanted to create calm around her to lock in a decision, a quality he found deeply attractive, if unnerving. She looked lovely in her white sundress.

You do realize you don't have to go, he said.

The crack in his voice made Alain wish he hadn't said what he said as soon as he'd said it.

Natasha sucked her teeth. Really, Alain? she said. Please let's not talk about this anymore. What's the alternative for me? Stay here with you until you get tired of me and leave me behind?

I'll ignore that provocation, he said. You know I will never leave you. You own me.

Alain smiled at this, for it was true. Despite her effort not to, Natasha smiled at this one truth they shared.

Stay, he continued. Together, we could turn the bookstore and all the other businesses I've started into something special. It won't be long before someone pays my father a lot of money for the store. We'll live in the big house. Have children . . .

You and your big business fantasies! They never stop, do they? They take too long to become reality.

Because they're realistic. Growth takes time. It's normal. It's normal in the US and Europe, too. So it should be normal here. Come on, you loved hanging out at the bookstore. I told you about that Canadian couple that was interested in buying it a few months back. Once we spruce it up, we'll get an even better price for it. I'll have the nest egg to set us up in Montreal or New York.

Those cities are too cold for me, she said.

Miami then. Even though I hate Miami.

I love Miami, though I've never been. I hear it's nice and small and warm.

It's also dirty. You have to drive too much there for me. There's a highway there, I-95. Almost every day you see a couple cars on the side of the road crunched up in ridiculous shapes after accidents. Sometimes I can't even figure out how the cars collided to produce those shapes. I suppose you could have fun there, turning those scenes into paintings. You love the macabre.

Even while blustering to buy time, Alain Destiné could tell he'd upset Natasha. She stiffened in her thin white dress, which had acquired a bluish tint from the first rays of the dawn sunlight. She hated the way he, like many people, spoke of art, especially her art, as though the work allowed them to read the artist. Like they knew her. Don't tell me what I love to do, she thought. Don't tell me about myself because part of you was aroused while taking in my art. The connection between the work produced and me, my heart, is never as simple and linear as you want it to be. Alain remembered the first lecture Natasha had given her about this: I create because I like to do it when I'm moved to do it, and it feels natural, funny. The colors and shapes flow through me. I create images and not words because I'm not interested in debate or discussion. I even know novelists who feel the same way. I bet most do. I could care less what you think of it. Experience it as romantic or macabre all you want, for sure, but keep your theories about it, and me, to yourself.

She didn't say all that to Alain this time, for she was tired and ready to move on with her life. Still . . .

You and that fucking nest egg, she said.

Yeah, that fucking nest egg, he said. You're an artist, baby. People don't have to know who you are or what you look like or even if you can speak English before they buy your work, invest in you. Me, I've been to other countries. I've seen life there. Jobs good enough to take care of a family are almost as hard to secure in lands of plenty when you're a foreigner as they are here. No one likes immigrants, especially your precious Europeans. Notice how I talk about jobs when it comes to life abroad while here I talk about creating organizations. Out there, I can't just go out, make shit up, and make a living. I can here.

You can do it anywhere, Alain, she said. You're the smartest man I know! A sound businessman. Let's go away and create something, a new organization, a new business. Whatever. Something. Let's just go. I can't believe we're having this argument again.

I can't leave Haiti again, Natasha, Alain said, suddenly fatigued. My life is here. This is my country. It's your country too, by the way. Haitians need you more than the Italians do. Stop acting like you don't know that.

Shhhh, not so loud, Natasha said.

I don't care if your husband hears me.

Why don't you want me to be happy?

Why do you have to leave me to be happy? Why can't you be happy with me here? Wait, you are happy with me here, if last night and this morning were an indication.

Natasha smiled.

It's not you, Alain, she said. It's me. It's this city, this country. I don't know how to explain it. They bring me down. I can't breathe here anymore.

Why?

I don't know why. Maybe I need to leave Haiti to understand why. It's hard to explain. I feel like nothing ever happens here. Or what happens here is not enough. We live. We suffer. We die. Prematurely. Suddenly. Passively.

That's how it goes for all mankind, Natasha.

But here, the sun shines and shines and shines. Then the sky rains and rains and rains. Only the stoic palm trees seem to be in on the joke, the incredible nothingness of this tropical sameness. The extremes of this country are just too much. They threaten to make me numb to novelty and invention. The joy of inspiration stopped existing here for me recently. I don't want to feel numb, but I do. I can't work and certainly can't live that way. From what I can tell, life here's been the same way since the beginning! Maybe I don't fit in to this society anymore. Maybe I don't want to fit in to this society anymore. Maybe I can't. Come on, Alain, you know what I'm talking about.

You're the only member of your entire class at College Bird who still lives in Haiti.

So fucking what? I'm happy here. The country's been good to me. More than generous. Can you imagine the obstacles our forefathers and mothers had to overcome to make sure we got the chance to exist in this room in this town this day? The Middle Passage across the Atlantic from Guinea and Benin, which meant weeks, if not months, of living in the bowels of too-small and too-crowded Dutch ships. Slavery. Centuries of slavery. The rebellion. Two decades of revolutionary war. The international embargoes. Two centuries of them shits. The American occupation. Two decades of that. The Duvaliers. Three decades of them. Post-Duvalier anarchy. Two decades and counting. We only know the other stuff from books. We are children of the anarchy era. Still, I bet you everyone from Haiti's previous eras would happily trade places with you for life in this Haiti, this so-called vacuum of originality. The so-called Republic of NGOs. How could Haiti be so devoid of inspiration when we fell in love here? What greater creation can a society allow, the freedom to love? Do you remember that day?

I don't want to, she said.

She looked down. Her toenails looked nice. Pink went well with her dark chocolate skin. She should cry, she told herself. Cry, Natasha. Cry, damn it. He deserved as much. He deserved to see you cry at least once for the pain you have caused him and will cause him further still this day.

Let him see that you hurt as much he does. For once. Just a little. It could be your good-bye gift to him. Oh no, what is he doing?

I told you I was almost ready for round four, Alain said.

Alain wrapped his arms around Natasha and cupped her breasts through her thin dress. She could feel his readiness and his forgiving smile without turning around. Natasha purred. Oh, baby, she said. The condoms are on the top shelf of my closet. Could you please go get them first?

Yes, Alain said. Though pregnancy would make a hell of a parting gift, he thought.

I can't find them, he said, once inside the closet. The room was large and empty and poorly lit. Its owner had clearly given up on it. Natasha didn't answer him. Instead he heard her close the closet door on him, then lock it, carefully, tenderly, as if she were closing a coffin.

What, what are you doing, Natasha? Alain said. Are you crazy?

I'm sorry, Alain, Natasha said. But I have to. I have to go.

Alain stood there in his bare feet with a rapidly shrinking erection, hands on his hips, mouth agape. He was a businessman, an expert at cost-benefit analysis. No cost-benefit analyst worth his salt would recommend he start screaming and pounding on the door from inside a married woman's closet in her bedroom in a palace under armed guard while her husband slept down the hall. No, I can't do that, he thought. Not even if I wasn't naked.

You're a real genius, Destiné. How could you overplay your hand so badly? How the hell did you end up trapped in a closet in another man's mansion with no clothes on? *Mon Dieu*, he thought. What a bitch.

He heard keys faintly jingle outside the closet. They had been tossed on the floor. He couldn't tell if they'd landed inside or outside the bedroom. Alain heard Natasha open the door leading out of her room into the hallway. The girlfriend who wouldn't have been his girlfriend if he'd been a wee bit less cocky walked out of her room without looking back. Alain would have felt her glance if she had. Three men swooped in to take her luggage. They did so silently. Then the bedroom door closed, and Alain knew he had been left alone with only the creaking sound of his breaking heart for company.

Eight hours later, a serene calm fell on the National Palace. For one of the rare times in its two-hundred-year history, the city seemed to be empty. Alain Destiné found his ability to coolly assess and deal with his situation fray. He sat on the floor and sobbed. The floor was carpeted and the carpet was plush. He felt like he was having a heart attack. He pressed his hand hard on his breast, as if trying to keep his heart from exploding out of his chest and through his eyes and nose. He could barely breathe. He felt dizzy. Alain tried to stand but his legs buckled under his weight. He fell to an elbow. A pop song's lyric wafted through his mind: "Be still my beating heart / It would be better to be cool." Last September, *Le Nouvelliste*, the Haitian newspaper of record, had praised Alain for his cool. The august daily named him among the young business leaders of the future of Haiti because he had successfully negotiated raises for workers at a Pepsi bottler in Léogâne, ending a strike.

Congratulations, Mr. Capitalist Tool, Natasha said when he sneaked into her bed that evening, wearing the stink of several celebratory drinks. You're really going to be popular in the business community after this move.

Alain ignored her sarcasm. He knew she was right. She was always right. His bosses were unhappy with the deal with the union. They hated the word "union." Politically, though, his reputation received a boost and a new dimension. Thanks to his feat, the government finally began to take a hard look at how it could better protect the country's workers. It began to explore setting up a national minimum wage policy and an agency to enforce it, a chairmanship job Alain was going to audition for at a parliamentary hearing scheduled for the next day. He was only twenty-five years old, a smooth talker in a nation of smooth talkers, armed with a hard-won MBA from New York University. He had been holding his own in a town overpacked with internationally educated bullshit artists far more seasoned than he was. He had already proved adept at cultivating good mentors in the local and international castes that ruled Port-au-Prince, including the president of the republic, Natasha's husband. His friends among the working-class people who did the hard work of trying to build and live in Haiti all year round kept faith in him too. Nothing had ever gone wrong for young master Destiné, not for long anyway, during his rise from anonymous son of an anonymous librarian from Place Boyer to potential industrialist and policymaker. He had no reason to believe it ever would. He got things done. That's what he did. He was a rare bird. Debilitating setbacks for other men were mere speed bumps for him. Winning was easy. It's my Destiné, went his lame pun about why his luck was so consistently good and his will and wits were so consistently winning.

Then there was the not-so-small matter of his affair with the artist Natasha Robert. She was an even rarer bird than he, for she came from a far more meager background than his to achieve a degree of success that was potentially greater than his. She displayed talent to become an artist and a celebrity unlike any seen in Haiti in a while, not since Father Métélus anyway. She took pleasure in illustrating Haitians' flirtations with self-destruction, chasing your own death, to paraphrase Freud, unlike most other local artists. She was almost ascetic about painting and sculpting visions of Haitians, Dante's circles of hell, and a forgiving, Haitian-looking Jesus. Her canvases used a lot of faded blues, greens, pinks, and yellows. "Provençal" was the word Alain had heard an international art dealer use to describe her style, as in reminiscent of the palettes used by Cézanne and other old-school painters from southern France. Natasha, of course, painted different subjects. Explicitly political and spiritual in theme, Natasha's paintings were disturbing, dealing with unironic notions of Haitian sanctity that countered or mocked every traditional narrative of the rise and fall of Haitian society by pointedly and repeatedly asking unsettling questions: Did Haitian society fall, as many development markers suggest, or is it on a heavenly trajectory? Is financial failure a sign of virtue? Isn't it inevitable that all rich people will go to hell? Aren't foreigners' reactions to Haiti proof of God's sense of humor? In the process, Natasha certified herself as nuts among the rich and as clever among the smart set. And the poor . . . stole her art whenever they could.

Natasha's focus on her work was impressive. Her only indulgence, as far as Alain could tell, was sleeping with him every couple of days since they'd met at a party for a new exhibit of some other artist at Cane A Sucre a few years earlier. Alain had trouble remembering who spoke to whom first, who made the first move, who said cool, all right, let's go. Did she choose him? Is that why she was able to let him go so easily? Should they have married?! Was that my cardinal sin? Could those words, of all things, have saved the day? She never told me she loved me either, but that was beside the point, wasn't it? She loved me. I inspired her work, the thing she cared about the most. Did I love her? Or did I simply want to beat the

President at the game of winning deeper feelings from his wife than he could, Haiti's oldest sport? Maybe. Maybe if you didn't play it so fucking cool, Destiné, too many fucking jokes, maybe if you told her you loved her, maybe she would have spurned her old man completely in your favor. Your victory would have been total. Maybe. And maybe not. Jeez. Alain, grow up. Could it ever have been so simple? It was so simple because you actually did love her. Face it. Alain, old chum, things did not go according to plan with this one because you had no plan for this one. Love was new ground to you, a foreign language you had yet to master. Just give up and move on. Your case over your rival could have been helped if you had a plan for her like you had a plan for everything else about your future. Jesus, Alain, you loved her, didn't you? said another voice inside his head. The case could have been made, Alain thought. He liked to believe he'd made it. Alain was not one for loose ends. They had an understanding, he thought. The old man would serve as a placeholder until he scored, or got on solid track for, the fortune to secure his and Natasha's future together. They had a deal! Unspoken, but such was the way of such deals since time immemorial, no? For the love of God, woman, what the hell did you want from me? We had a deal. Should I have spoken the unspoken?

At this thought, Alain Destiné got off the ground and started looking around for a key, anything, to get him out of the closet of the National Palace that hot afternoon.

He suspected a key had to exist, but tumbling cement bricks of sadness had pummeled him into wasting the day. You can be such a loser sometimes, Alain. The darkness of the closet was thick and inky and closed in on him. Sunlight leaked through the bottom of the door from the bedroom, humming a faint hymn. Empty clothes hangers click-clacked and hissed this way and that as his arm slid between them. He tapped and tapped the walls in hopes of uncovering a light switch, a key, a window, a . . . door-knob?

The door opened into a stairwell. A humming light-bulb greeted him. Its dim light was surrounded by flies and the smell of a thousand pairs of old sneakers. The fuzzy light left the stairwell dangerously too dark, but down the rabbit hole Alain went anyway. Maybe this secret stairwell was created by a prudent former president of the republic who wanted his wife and children to have an escape route out of the palace if an unruly mob came calling. They did have a tendency to do that around here. Or maybe the stairwell merely served as a pathway for maids and servants to flit about their duties to the first family even more invisibly than tradition called for. The stairwell was lit no better than the locked closet, but it had a railing, which Alain grabbed with both hands to keep from falling. Alain used the railing to guide his descent and maintain a sense of balance, which was rendered fragile by the assault of the afore-mentioned horrid smell. A surprise burst of euphoria from his escape from that infernal closet excited him. So did a keen sense of what his next move had to be. Alain began to skip down the stairs, two, then three steps at a time. His enthusiasm for his next move, which had leapt swiftly from musing to concrete and urgent action plan, mounted. He will race to the airport! That's what he'll do. He will race to the airport and talk his way through to the tarmac, where the President and Natasha would hopefully be stalled for one reason or another. He will then speak New York English to persuade the peacekeepers to part and let him reach the first couple. I'm his nephew, he'd say. I have one last message to give the President. It's from his mother. Part, the sea of stupid blue helmets will. Then he will reach the President and his wife. The sun will be hot, but the tarmac will be hotter. Heavy fumes and heat will have everyone wondering if his presence was a hallucination. Natasha will briefly set aside her typically bored artist pose. Her shift in spirit will be visible mainly to him, a man who has evoked it before, after either eloquently working his tongue between her legs or making her laugh with such abandon at an off-color joke or a bit of tickling that she snorted like a hog and her eyes danced.

Destiné, the President will say, on guard.

The President will try to play it cool, indifferent even, because noblesse oblige is the President's signature move. To what do I owe this grand and very surprising visit from Haiti's best and brightest? he'll say. Have you already completed your work turning our economy into Sweden's?

The President's right hand will, no doubt, disappear into the folds of the pocket in which he kept the small gun he'd told Alain he always had on him. I even sleep with it, the President once confided. Alain couldn't tell if he was joking or not. Probably not. The President will no doubt shoot me in the forehead, Alain thought, if I make a sudden move or if he is struck by the reasonable impulse to murder the man who has been sleeping with his wife. After putting me down like a dog, the President, of course, will turn to the blue helmets and tell them and other shocked witnesses that I was an assassin he had been warned about by the government's intelligence services, as if the country these days had any of those things, a functional government and intelligent public services.

I will avoid this unwanted scenario by greeting him most cheerfully, Alain thought. Mr. President, I'll say, in the firm but eager tone of a military man submitting to his master. Then I will take Natasha by both hands and turn her to face me while keeping her positioned between the President and me. If he lost his head, he would have to shoot her to shoot me. I think I could count on him to not do that. Not at that moment anyway. Natasha, I will say, with as deep and heroic a voice as I can muster. Shit, what should I say?

I will quote Dante, her favorite author:

There was no hymning of Bacchus or Apollo but of
    three persons in the divine nature, the divine and
    human natures in one person
The singing and the dancing were completed
and those holy lights seemed to turn to us
happy to pass from one care to another
then that light which had narrated to me the
    marvelous life of the poor man of God
broke the silence of those concordant powers
and said: "Since one lot of corn has been winnowed
    and since the seed has been stored away, sweet love
    invites me to thresh the other."

Then I hope I will have the courage to look her in the eyes and say: I love you, baby. All that matters is that we be in the same room, house, bed, together, forever, 'til death do us part. Nothing else matters to me. Not Haiti, not my family, not pacifism, not the end of unemployment, torture, infant deaths, malnutrition, or illiteracy. Fuck all that. Let me know where you land in Tuscany as soon as you can. I'll come to you on the next plane to Italy, and then we'll run away and go start our family wherever else. Even if we have to run away to Papua New Guinea to do so in peace, I won't give a fuck. I'll be the happiest man alive as long as I'm with you. OK?

Yes, she'll say.

I'll nod to her. Then I'll turn to the President and say, Have a safe trip, Mr. President, sir.

I'll say so with utmost sincerity. Then I'll turn around and walk, briskly, away from them and into the bosom of peacekeepers and their gob-smacked faces before disappearing into the crowds inside the airport.

With that inspiring thought of swashbuckling gallantry, Alain Destiné completed his naked run down the secret stairwell of the National Palace and burst through a heavy metal door and into the cement-floored backyard. *Merde, je suis nue*, he realized. As he caught his breath and covered up his immodesty, a heavier-than-expected silence drew his attention. Downtown Port-au-Prince felt oppressively hot. Steam rose from the asphalt between his toes. There were no security guards or soldiers around, even in the parking lot. The buzzing voices of cell phone sellers, money traders, urchins begging a few meters beyond the tall barbwire wall bordering the back of the palace, seemed stilled. As though time itself had been frozen. He fought through what felt like the loudest pregnant pause in history and ran to his car, a ten-year-old Chevy, rusty red, with a black leather interior he liked to keep shiny, an absurd, small indulgence that gave him immense pleasure. The car was so uncool to just about everyone else in Port-au-Prince that he never feared someone would steal it, even during the city's occasional waves of carjacking frenzy. So he often left it unlocked. There, in a garment bag in the trunk, lay his backup suit. Thank God he never left home without a backup of his favorite uniform, a dark jacket and trousers only a very trained eye would recognize as unmatched, and a white shirt. Maybe he won't wear a tie today. No time to waste on a Windsor knot.

He ambled the car out onto rue St. Honoré. The time, late afternoon, was a rare one for him to be leaving the National Palace. Since his girlfriend had moved in there a couple of months ago, he entered and left mainly in the wee hours, like a thief, though he felt as if he was the only person to lose something after each clandestine visit. Traffic on rue St. Honoré was light. Even foot traffic. A bank of narrow, aluminum-roofed shacks in varying shades of green featured their usual array of activities. One was a restaurant. Next door, an old man sold soda. The ubiquitous cell phone dealer stood under a red umbrella. They are the new cocaine, these cell phones, Alain thought. If prostitution is the oldest profession, telecommunications is the newest profession. Natasha was right. I need to get my head into these new businesses. A huge woman with broad shoulders swept away dirty rainwater trapped in the backed-up manhole in front of her house. She did it so determinedly. Her face wore the gravest concentration. The two girls jumping rope around her should be more careful, Alain thought. Their mother spent so much energy sweeping the floor she seemed to have none left to keep an eye on her bored daughters playing in one of the busiest streets in one of the most crowded cities on earth. All that garbage. Her broom was too small.

The way the house then toppled onto the woman and

the girls happened in slow motion. Alain saw the house and the house next to it and the house next to that one and most of the other houses on the street tumble onto the street, the people, and the passing cars. The odd thing was that Alain Destiné found himself watching houses fall and people die while high off the ground. His car was . . . flying. What the fuck! Alain's car had been catapulted into the Caribbean sky by an invisible and powerful force. The force had turned his Chevy into a flying carpet of sorts, a rusty red Haitian-American combo of the sort of magical melding of adventurous and funky transport mechanism that had tickled him pink in the stories of Arabian nights his father read to him as a child. From the sky, strangely, Port-au-Prince looked uncommonly beautiful. He hadn't visited Paris yet, but surely Paris couldn't be as beautiful as his hometown, this jewel of the Caribbean, this diamond in the rough, when viewed from the driver's seat of a car launched two hundred meters above sea level. Awesome. Natasha, he thought, I have got to show her this.

During the car's descending arc, death jabbed Alain in the ribs.

Oh my God!, Alain screamed. He saw the National Palace collapse into itself like a wedding cake stepped on by an invisible giant toddler.

Oh. My. God.

He gripped the steering wheel as the car nose-dived toward the earth.

THE COWARD

When Natasha Robert began walking up the stairs to the private jet minutes before the earthquake, hand in paw with her husband, she looked like she was walking slowly. In truth, she was being dragged. Gently and discreetly, but pulled against her will all the same. Her resistance was palpable to her husband. She felt like the puppy the President had had as a boy, the one he found wounded on a dusty road one morning and was determined to nurse to health and keep happy for no damn reason other than the belief that a puppy this cute deserved a better life than the one fate had on the table. Eventually the boy who would become president and the bleeding stray dog had tugs-of-war all the same, mainly when the boy was ordered to kick the dog outside so he could do his homework. Accustomed to his owner and savior's love, the dog grew scared of the world outside the house. He rarely ventured outside without his master, so getting him to go out and have fun was a chore the President took pleasure in. At Toussaint Louverture Airport, five minutes before the devastating quake, the president of Haiti interpreted his new bride's resistance as a replay of his beloved Fox's bad case of nerves. Like that puppy, few things had ever worked out for this girl in her young life in this country where few things, if anything, ever worked properly, except for love and death. (Tax collecting didn't work; trust him, he tried.) Not that the President felt he should be held even partially responsible for this tragic state of affairs. We inherited a bad hand and are doing the best we can with it. That's the only explanation he had for Haiti's seemingly unstoppable decline from the pearl of the Caribbean during the colonial era to the poorest country in the Western Hemisphere postindependence. In his sixty years, he had yet to hear a better explanation.

The President stepped down a few steps to retrieve his nervous bride, reaching first for the tips of her fingers. Her hands were appealingly soft but wet with sweat. They were clammy and cold too. Natasha looked smaller and browner than usual, but she was still beautiful. So gorgeous, in fact, that his heart skipped a beat when she returned his gaze. After all these months he was as surprised as anyone by how she still took his breath away each time her eyes met his. His cheeks felt flush. He wished this would stop happening. Will it ever? I'll have the rest of my life to find out, he thought, a thought that made the old man turn serious.

We should get going, he said. Let me tell you a story.

Natasha Robert and the President were now standing in the shadow of the jet, which was embossed with a giant American flag. The President stood on a step so he could be the same height as Natasha and look her in the eyes. The soldiers who had escorted them to the tarmac of Toussaint Louverture Airport were off a ways, standing under the airport tower's shade, chatting among themselves. His posse kept a respectful distance. They knew not to be close enough to eavesdrop but he knew they heard every word anyway. These people had ears like bats.

I know what you're thinking, the President said. Long pause. Natasha looked up in surprise and pursed her lips. She wished she could melt into the asphalt.

What? she said. What did you say?

I just wanted to let you know that I understand how you feel, the President said. Back when I was your age, I got terrified when my dreams were on the verge of coming true too. Here's how I developed the ability to overcome this fear. When I was a boy, my father used to take me fishing in a corner of the Artibonite River. My father was a farmer from Hinche who was said to own no land. My mother was a laundry woman. I didn't care. Like every boy, I loved to hang out with my father without my siblings or mother around. Those mornings, honey-gold sunbeams bathed the green waters around us. The smell of jasmine enveloped us. Back then there were trees on the banks of the river in the country's breadbasket. The trees were tall, leafy, and proud. Their branches and leaves opened their palms up to the heavens to drink in the sun's life-giving rays with *ivresse*. The trees looked like they were praying. Photosynthesizing with God. The millions of people, small and needy, who reaped the benefits of the trees' constant prayers knew well enough to thank the earth and God regularly for their existence.

My father and I ambled down to the river most often on mornings when it was too hot for me to play football with my friends and too early for him to have worked through the night's hangover. We sat in his small boat for hours. My father often slept during this time, but with his eyes open. I stared at the schools of fish swimming around us in the still river, and I imagined I had a machine gun to speed up their conquest. On days when I had problem that needed sorting, I asked my father for advice. I was a shy child. I stammered a lot. But, strangely, not when I spoke to my papa. I told Papi of a kid in school who I thought was a friend but who hurt my feelings by making fun of me. Recently, he had started taunting me by calling me Garcia, my middle name. In front of all our classmates, he kept saying that my name was Dominican and that I wasn't really Haitian. I was a traitor, a spy. All the kids laughed at me. I hated it. I am Haitian, Papa, right? I said. I'm not a traitor, right? I would never hurt people. What was this boy talking about, Papa? I'm not Dominican, right? Even I was, all Dominicans are not spies and enemies, are they?

What should I do about this boy? He bothers me non-stop, Papa. I'm starting to lose concentration in class.

What?! my father said, startled awake. He coughed and wiped his mouth with his shirtsleeve. He wore that pained look he got whenever he was confronted with unpleasant news. My father always looked like he was easily wounded, for he was a thin man. Thin eyes, lips, hands, legs, and torso. People in our *quartier* called him Chinaman. The women loved him. They wanted to cradle his waifish frame. They liked his easy, lopsided grin. His head was clean-shaven yet gray at the temples. Raffish and handsome and somnolent, that was my father, the latest in a long line of easy-to-love men in our family that ended with me.

What is the boy's name? my father asked me that day in the boat. B–B–B–Bernard, I said. Bernard Métélus.

Métélus's boy? he said. You letting that little runt get to you? What's wrong with you, son? Did you punch him in his face after he insulted you? Did you punch him and tell him that Dominicans and Haitians don't exist? It's one damn island, one country of people stuck on an island in the middle of the Caribbean Sea. We're the same squirrels trying to get nuts from the same stingy bastards.

Non, papa, I said.

Good, Papa said. What a fucking fool, that Métélus kid. Just like his father. Still. You're better off keeping that to yourself. Better to make friends than enemies with him. Don't let that anti-Dominican shit get to you, son. I gave you that name for a reason. The Dominicans are all right. Don't let the loudmouths fool you. That doesn't mean they don't have their funny ways. Not too long ago, they had a president, Rafael Trujillo, a real asshole, who, on a whim, ordered his army to execute the Haitian population living in the borderlands we share with them. In a few months, the Dominicans killed somewhere between twenty to thirty thousand of us. Probably more. No one can ever tell how many Haitians are in any one place at a given time. We're everywhere! Anyway, the Dominicans really got carried away with themselves that day. The soldiers used knives and swords. They didn't spare women or children. You see, some Dominicans never got over the fact that their people are Haitian. African, Indian, with a dash of European. Haitian. The island was one country for a long time, for a longer time than it's been artificially separated by the Americans. The propaganda that keeps us separated is ridiculous. Oh, we don't share everything. Over there, they have a thing for Christopher Columbus that's pretty embarrassing. No one else in the hemisphere likes that motherfucker. We prefer to celebrate the people who stood up to the Spanish conquistadors. Here, we love our African soul. Not in the DR. They love their Spanish roots. It's no big deal. To each his own God be true, right? However, being mad at sharing our ancestry is like being mad at being called human. The human condition has no mysteries for us Haitians, does it, son? We take its best and its worst, with a shrug and a chuckle and a glass of rum. We're tough hombres, foolish, maybe a wee bit crazy from the sun and sex, but we have good taste. We take the best shots from God and the devil on any given day and still we rise. My father chuckled. I didn't understand all of what he was talking, but I got the gist of it.

The Dominicans called the massacre El Corte, the cut. The sad event was also known as the Parsley Massacre from stories people told about how the soldiers made sure they killed defenseless Haitians and not defenseless Dominicans by accident—ah, the complications of fratricide. Trujillo had the soldiers hold up parsley sprigs to their potential victims and then ask them, What is this? If the potential victim said the word "parsley" with the wrong accent, off went her head. To illustrate the absurdity of it all, my father then said the word "parsley" with pitch-perfect Spanish and the widest, toothiest grin. A bit of drool dribbled down the corner of his mouth.

Natasha, I could care less about history, not now and definitely not back then, the President said, holding Natasha's gaze as steadily as he held her hands. In my teenage mind, the moral of the story he told me revolved around the magical powers of immortality conveyed from knowing the right way to say the right word, like "parsley," at the right time. You could say my political career was born that day. I became a listener. I became a diplomat of sorts, a reconciler and not a fighter. A crowd-pleaser. A shit-eater. A winner. I got off that boat and went back to the neighborhood determined to become Métélus's best friend. I wasn't going to ask him to stop mocking me. I was going to make him like me so much that mocking me would come to seem a waste of his time. I was going to become useful to him, you see. And it worked! I rode his coattails to the presidency! Everyone wants to be liked and served, especially bullies. I didn't want to be coddled by everyone like my father was, but I figured being inoffensively offensive in aggressive and hostile surroundings would spare me the worst of any situation. I was not a quiet boy or a choirboy. I could fake humor like the best of men. On my journey to manhood, I simply found the easiest way to eliminate obstacles was to listen, then seduce. Just so. Never too much. Too much of anything, especially words, ruined events, moments, made life unnecessarily harder. Live in the moment, but without excess. Have faith, have cool, have a ready modest smile. So when Métélus became president of Haiti, I was his right-hand man.

Some of the people who were about to die during the massacre realized immediately what the murderous Dominican was asking of them with the parsley sprig facing them, father said. They would say the word the wrong way, realize their mistake, then try again quickly to get it right before the first blow fell on them. Sometimes they tried after the second or third blow too. It was always too late. There was no mercy to be had. You cannot take words back after they've been spoken, son, my father said. In my long life, I've seen his advice hold up well over the years. So, baby, as you embark on this adventure with me and you feel your nerves getting the best of you, just do what I do when I get confronted by a scary situation.

What's that? Natasha said.

I say the word "parsley," the President said. Over the years, the word became part incantation and part reminder for me to stay calm and careful in situations where most of my friends or competitors would panic. It was a way to remind myself that whatever odd situation I had gotten myself into was of my own creation and thus it was amply manageable. Natasha, sweetheart, you should have faith that much of the same is true for you. There is nothing bad that is going to happen to you as long as you are with me as we move around this planet. There's no threat that you won't have the power to handle whether you're with me or not. Your will to power got you this far in life. I doubt you'll face anything worse than the things you had to overcome already.

In her heart, she knew he was right. Natasha felt her spirit swell with strength that she did not think she was capable of feeling. You really think so? she said, immediately regretting the girlish pitch in her voice.

I do believe you will be fine, my love, he said. As long as you repeat the magic word after me.

What's that?

Parsley, he said.

Before she could react, his phone rang. The ringtone was unfamiliar to her. High-pitched. The President's face grew dark. He turned away from her. A first. He usually liked to have her witness as he conducted the affairs of the state.

A lot of people on the streets think us politicians are all crooks, he used to say. How could the people in charge of a country so poor have politicians as corrupt as vultures? What do they think we're robbing? The place has nothing, absolutely nothing. So to prove the sincerity of my intentions, the President said during their courtship, I will be totally transparent with my business. You will see that I'm not a crook. I am conflict-averse and a terrible public speaker, but I am not a plundering president of Haiti like some of my predecessors. Not that I'm a saint or anything. But by the time I got to office, the national cupboard was basically empty. I hope you come to understand the limits of the powers of my office, of our nation. I hope you could grow to trust me.

Natasha thought the man was crazy. Still, his generous and probably dangerous gestures had the desired effect on her. She grew to appreciate the privilege of bearing witness to the politics of their country as they happened in real time. Haiti's sad state sickened her and made her want to flee the island in disgust more than ever. The place was a wreck, and Natasha was in no mood to be fascinated or philosophical about it. The view from a front-row seat in the President's office freaked her out instead of giving her the more common frisson of a rubbernecker. So now for the first time, as her commitment to him was about to reach a fraught climax, he wanted to keep a piece of his business secret from her. She was not going to let him. She walked up behind him and stopped just short enough to eavesdrop on his conversation.

Yes, Mr. President, he said.

Mr. President? she thought. This was the first time she had heard him speak English and call another person Mr. President. He had to be talking to the American president. That's the only other president he's ever referred to. Wow.

To be honest, a big part of me feels relieved, sir, he said. You really believe my people will be proud of me for doing this? I'm impressed by how well you understand the Haitian people, sir. I'm sure the American people would also be proud to learn one morning that their president had overnight chosen to retire to the Italian countryside instead of serving their interests until the end of his mandate. You don't have to threaten me, sir. I was just making a joke. I am fully aware of the fact that your predecessor had my predecessor exiled to Africa and banned from ever entering the Western Hemisphere. The Central African Republic. Not somewhere nice like Egypt or Gabon. Right. Yes. I understand. Italy is a much nicer place for me to start a family. I'll have a nice trip, sir. Thanks for taking time from your busy . . . Mr. President? Mr. President? Mr. President?

Who was that? Natasha said.

The boss, he said.

Who?

Who do you think? the President snapped. What, you didn't think your president had a boss? I do. Everyone does. Even you do.

Even your boss does, Natasha said.

The President looked curiously at his new bride, then he trudged on. They walked up the steps to the airplane. Halfway up, the President tossed his cell phone away. He didn't throw away the device in anger but did so softly, wearily. He was letting go of the unmentionable every-things it represented, did, and had him do. He was too tired from years of hating most of it to muster rage. He watched the black phone fly through the humid air. Suddenly, he found himself flying toward the phone. He found himself floating in the air away from the plane, horizon-tally, like Superman. The President looked like a fat, bald, nattily suited beach ball soaring through the sky between the sun and an undulating sea of asphalt. He didn't know what caused this to happen. He knew the landing on the tarmac's asphalt, whenever it occurred, was going to hurt like hell. The force of his momentum was such that his tie smacked him dead in the eye. His eyes watered. Now that, that really pissed him off.

Merde, the President said.

His jaw was the first part of his body to hit the ground.

PART III

If *sub specie aeternitatis* there is no reason to believe that anything matters, then that doesn't matter either, and we can approach our absurd lives with irony instead of heroism and despair.

—Thomas Nagel, "The Absurd"

LOOKING FOR A NEEDLE IN THE RUBBLE

Outside an isolated tent a hundred meters from hundreds and thousands of newly planted tents for earthquake victims in Port-au-Prince, two doctors, one American and the other French, had a cigarette before starting their workdays. It was six a.m., a couple of days after the quake. In most countries not located in the middle of the Caribbean Sea, there would be a slight chill in the air at that hour. In Haiti, the temperature was perfect, not too hot, not cool, just right. The doctors felt good in their skins. This bothered them. Life shouldn't feel this good when death was so spectacularly random and massive around them. They smoked nervously. In the evening after dinner, they will drink heavily.

They say the first seventy-two hours are your best chance of finding survivors after disasters like this, the man, a Frenchman, said. In Banda Aceh, they found practically no one after forty-eight hours.

I know, an unmistakably American woman said. We got to Pakistan four days after their big one. There were no survivors.

None?

Zip. Zilch. Nada.

Putain. The poor bastards.

Inside the tent, which the doctors thought to be a storage tent, for it was the only tent with an armed guard standing in front of it at all times, the subconsciousness of a sleeping earthquake survivor filtered their analysis. Natasha Robert sprang awake. She was alert and amped, as if one of the doctors had extinguished his cigarette directly in her eye. She foraged around for her clothes, but all she could find were a pair of white tennis sneakers.

What the . . . ? Natasha stormed out of her tent wearing nothing but a white T-shirt and those tennis shoes, trailed by a startled bodyguard calling out, Madame! Madame! while stumbling and struggling to keep up with her long-legged strides. Before long, Natasha was lost in a maze of tents. They were blue or green, the color of mud or the color of eggshells. Some even had potted yellow flowers outside their zippered doors. Where is he? she said over her shoulder to the bodyguard, who was too out of breath to answer. To a group of intimidated soldiers coming toward her, she said, Have you seen my husband?

No, Madame, said the commander. Who is your husband?

What the hell?

She stalked off in another direction, down another row of tents. Kitchen staff, humanitarians, and other denizens of the camp parted like the Red Sea when they saw the determined, barely dressed Natasha stomping their way with her hair sticking out like antennas, shattering the delicate matinal, disturbing congregating ghosts.

At the base's hospital, Natasha stopped and gasped. There were dozens of wounded people seated on the ground. A line of them stood in front of a doctor, a nurse, and an administrator, who were already sweating from the rising heat and the workload. She saw the doctor fail to stifle a wince each time a child's scream came from inside the hospital, a clinic, which, in truth, was closer to the size of a gas station's bathroom. The nurse took note of each patient's complaints, though all of their problems were visible to the naked eye. A half-crushed head or shoulder, a mangled leg, a severed arm. Children of all sizes cried and whimpered all over the place, like a chorus, from pains that were too hard to look at and too painful for everyone, including the stunned parents and guardians, to keep a brave face in front of. Arms aloft, these parents offered the children to the doctors with the desperation of people making offerings to gods.

Humbled by this sight, Natasha turned away. The man she was looking for—her husband—turned out to be a few meters away with a concerned but clear-eyed look in his face. She saw her new bodyguard briefing the President. The President's face went from frown to smile when his eyes met Natasha's. His smile, she thought, was one of forgiveness for the scene she had caused in their funereal new neighborhood. They embraced warmly. His generosity made her regret her next words even though she said them with resolve.

I have to go, she said.

Where? The city is not safe. There are still aftershocks, buildings falling. We don't know . . .

I have to find Alain, she said, quickly adding, He's like a brother to me, the only family I have left.

But you don't know—

He's alive. I know.

She wanted to add: I can feel his soul's glow within my own. It burns in our world still. If it had been extinguished, I would know. Because we are one, two sides of the same coin, alpha and omega. One true love. I was stupid to deny this truth before for reasons that never held water when confronted with our passion. The only way I can justify my new lease on life after the cataclysm that we have miraculously survived is by giving all my love to the only person it belonged to all this time, or at the very least by bidding him a more proper farewell than the one I attempted before the earthquake. It's the right thing to do.

Natasha Robert didn't say any of those things to her husband when he took a step back to appraise her while holding both her shoulders. She tried to appear sweet and innocent. He seemed to buy her act. OK, he said, you can go, but you have to adhere to all our new security rules. They're for your own protection.

Of course, she said. The zing of nervous triumph she felt in her heart should have been tempered by the look her husband exchanged with her bodyguard. Bobo was his name. He was not dressed like a United Nations peacekeeper because he was not one. Bearish and bearded, Bobo belonged to an older school of friends of the President who Natasha rarely met, the kind whose jovial manner hid a tendency to protect their friend's interests by any means necessary, few of them kind.

By the time their bulletproof SUV exited the gates of the spontaneous settlement near Toussaint Louverture Airport she refused to call home, she stood poised to enter the choppy streets of Port-au-Prince for the first time since the earth beneath her feet had rioted. Natasha was wide-eyed and anxious but her mind and heart were clear. Her first glimpse of a toppled house gave her no pause as she nibbled absentmindedly on a croissant and sipped orange juice from a plastic cup. The croissant was buttery and flakey, and the glass of OJ was freshly squeezed and slightly bitter. This nice breakfast was courtesy of a female French soldier or humanitarian—is there really a difference?—who had come to her tent after her husband gave a signal. The lady also brought her new green cargo pants, a clean white V-neck T-shirt, and aviator sunglasses. She didn't need the glasses. The earthquake seemed to have dislodged the painterly reverie with which she used to see the world and replaced it with a desire to see things as they were. The Haiti in front of her looked extraordinarily vivid. All her senses felt fired-up. For once, her world seemed made of flesh and blood and not just souls, devils and angels, colors, canvas, palettes, puns, and hymns. We are all swimming upstream. We're all saints and sinners, she'd thought over and over again in her cool and dark tent the previous couple of days. We will all be forgiven. History probably forgot about us the minute we started thinking about her. The idea that history was worthless and tomorrow was for suckers caressed her. She did not know how the thought came to her. She understood that many things were destroyed by the quake, and that we will have to make what we need out of the rubble of the existence we have left. Or not. Live what life we have left and leave the rest to God. Lost in thought, Natasha paid no mind to Bobo. He was sitting in the front seat of the car, next to the driver. He could have been polishing, loading, and reloading guns, which he was. She could have cared less. Until he ordered the driver to turn left.

No, she said, turn right. We're going to the Palais.

She couldn't wait to introduce her new self to Alain, a man she had no reason to believe was still alive. This new Natasha would replace the one Alain knew, she thought, the one who needed men to take care of her because the process of creating art was the only thing in her life she felt confident enough to control and develop.

The President told me your friend lived in Place Boyer, Bobo said.

She thought the conversation was over. Her order was given.

No, Mr. . . . Bobo, is it? We're going to the Palais area, because, uh, my friend was at work near there when the earthquake came.

OK. But it's not wise to spend too much time in that area. It's the heart of the disaster and very dangerous. Right? Bobo said to the driver.

Right, the driver said, confused, but playing along anyway.

Why would the Champ de Mars be more dangerous than usual? Natasha asked.

We, we, don't know, Bobo said. The Americans told us it was. They said people there were desperate and could resort to attacking us. They said there may have been some looting.

Really?

The Americans said so.

And no one else?

And no one else.

Right. Tell me, Bobo, how do you know the President? You seem like old friends.

Bobo smiled.

Oui, *Madame*, *le Président* was a good friend of my father's. I've known him since I was a boy.

How nice, she said.

I'm hoping he takes us with him when you leave. This place is in bad shape. You're still moving, right? Right?

Natasha didn't answer. She wasn't sure of the answer. She didn't think it was any of his business either way.

During goudou-goudou, Bobo continued, without prompting, I had just gotten home after work and was standing in my garden with my arms wide open as my girl Diana and my son Nelson ran towards me. They are very affectionate children, like their mother was. Then the ground started shaking and literally threw them at me. I clutched them and we all fell down backwards. The house and the front porch exploded and landed right at my shoes. I tried to get up with the children but I couldn't. The shaking wouldn't stop. My feet kept sliding around, like I was ice-skating. I resorted to crawling away from the house with them. The earth hit me in the jaw repeatedly. Heavyweight champion punches, let me tell you. Somehow I managed to make it to my car. The quaking stopped and I drove off wildly. I came to the airport because I knew the President was here.

You mentioned your wife in past tense, Natasha said.

Yes, goudou-goudou killed her. The children told me she was setting the dinner table with Naomi our maid when they ran out of the house to greet me. I hope we leave the country soon. The kids deserve better than this. There's nothing left for us here.

Natasha avoided directly facing the blues in Bobo's lin-

gering gaze. But her scrim of aplomb began to fray anyway. Whether it would hold up in the face of the blues of
millions of Bobos now existing in Port-au-Prince, only
God knew. She didn't like the odds. She resumed staring
at the new Port-au-Prince, which forlornly stared back at
her under the mounting blaze of a bright morning sun.
The car ambled south on Boulevard Toussaint Louverture. The streets were strangely quiet. The air was still.
Traffic was light. The few people Natasha saw were sitting on the sidewalks with ashy arms and legs and dumbfounded looks on their faces. In the direction of Lalue on
rue Nazon, she saw the first of dozens of cars buried under
the rubble of tumbled buildings. Then she saw her first
looter. He was a boy, maybe eight, maybe ten years old.
He was reed-thin, with sickly reddish hair. Wearing a red
tank top with a white cross on it, blue shorts, and broken
sandals, he carried a full-to-the brim grocery bag half his
size and shuffled down the sidewalk quickly, anxiously
looking over his shoulders. When the crowd following
the boy emerged, crackling with noisy and nervous energy and carrying what looked like ill-gotten goods, Natasha, the driver, and Bobo all said *merde* in unison. To her
surprise, Natasha screamed, Stop the car! She opened the
car door quickly and told the boy to get in, fast. He did.

You're crazy, Bobo said. What are you doing? It's
against UN rules to give rides to nonstaff. Get him out of
here. He can only bring us trouble.

What are you talking about? Natasha said. You don't

work for the UN. Driver, the boy is strapped in. Go! Go! Go!

And he went. The SUV steamed through potholes and picked up speed even as the crowd came closer. The crowd paid the car no mind. These were the able and the hungry and the newly homeless. Like the first humans, after being cast out of heaven. If they couldn't eat or drink it, and no one had a gun pointed at them for trying to eat and drink (and, later, fuck), they couldn't be bothered. Natasha imagined that, like her, each one of them had a loved one in need who was lost in the pulverized concrete wilderness whom they hoped to find and bring medicine, food, water, and love to. She gave the boy the rest of her croissant and OJ. He gulped them without hesitation or saying *merci*. Nazon was a very wide boulevard. People were everywhere, carrying stuff that was too big and heavy for them to carry. The SUV had to slow down. Threading around looters and invalids was like tiptoeing around on a beach made of broken beer bottles. The boy they had picked up got nervous, squirmed, and, when Natasha reached out to him, bolted out of the moving car, still holding his bounty tightly. He ran back up Nazon without looking over his shoulder.

These are different times, Bobo told Natasha. People don't want to look back anymore. They can't. Too scary. They want the future.

The earthquake was like a big bang, Natasha thought. And we're scattered stars. She was crestfallen. Was she trying to hold on to a world that didn't exist anymore? As had happened to her often whenever she felt out of touch with where and who she was, she thought of Alain.

A tabula rasa, that's what I am, she mused. Like the canvases you face every morning, Alain would have said. The car turned west on Avenue John Brown and began crawling toward Champ de Mars and the National Palace, post-earthquake ground zero. The car stopped for long stretches of time. Two days after the quake, the authorities and international helpers hadn't had enough time to give everyone in the Champ de Mars area tarps and tents and sanitary and security facilities. A new city of homeless and seemingly nationless Haitians had grown around the national monuments. Right now the national square that was Champ de Mars looked like the world's largest hospital emergency room. It was not the first time that Natasha, a native of nearby Fort National, had seen over a million people congregated there. A greater number ended up there at the end of every float's parade every February during Carnival. Those teeming, sweaty people, too, were often half-naked and wearing red and blue in the form of red-and-blue handkerchiefs tied around the head, red-and-blue skirts around bouncing hips, red-and-blue shirts draped over the shoulders but rarely worn around glistening, muscular torsos, and red-and-blue capes (capes were big among the men come Carnival time) for shoulders both broad and malnourished. Red and blue were the colors of the national flag, and they were creatively twisted and crafted in all sorts of fashionable ways. This day the red she saw and quickly yearned to forget belonged to the blood of earthquake survivors barely surviving. Blood ran from every body part you could imagine. Rivers of the stuff. Why hadn't it all dried up by now, oh Lord? Maybe the blood was dry. Maybe it was the open, unbandaged wounds on all those bodies glistening under the hot and bright sun that made the blood look so fucking red. So fresh, so not clean. She saw red, but it was the blue that made her weep. People were crying for help. People were crying from pain. People were crying from grief. People were crying from the sight of other people crying. People cried out of rage. In the front seat, Bobo was horrified and kept talking to the people on the streets to calm his nerves, even though they couldn't hear him.

Why doesn't somebody move that dead child's body away from her crippled mother? he screamed. Can't they see she can't move? Can't they see what seeing what her baby looks like is doing to her?

Natasha saw one tragic tableau after another, and words failed her. She couldn't emit a single sound. She tried to tell the driver to drive faster, to get her away from a scene by escaping to another street. But the street had disappeared a long time ago. People were everywhere, suffering, not smiling. And they swirled and froze in a constant, random, awesome, and horrible traffic-clogging movie, causing the SUV to move at a glacial pace, if it moved at all, for hours. Natasha felt like a tourist in her own city being guided through an open-air museum of pain and despair. If the driver's name is Virgil, I'll kill myself, she thought. Her eyes took in grotesqueries her mind instantly wanted to forget. When she turned her head elsewhere in search of a balm, her eyes invariably landed on an even sadder sight. Then all three of them saw a sizable green garden. Their battered spirits were so grateful to see the color of life free from ruined brown bodies they took a while to notice the caved-in white building looming behind the lawn. The National Palace. It really was destroyed.

History was not her thing, nor was patriotism, but Natasha felt a loss of something dear and big and common to all Haitians at the sight of the seat of her country's leadership destroyed, with its guts spilling out on a grassy knoll. This should not have been allowed to happen, was an immediate thought. This is how much God hates the Republic of Haiti, was another. A building that had stirred passions to the point of madness in the hearts of some of the world's greatest emperors, from Napoleon to Woodrow Wilson, recalcitrant peasants, stentorian poets, sensitive singers, and conniving nation-builders and rebels over centuries was laid low by a random and brief belching of the earth. Oddly for a first lady, the loss of her home, which also happened to be a potent fetish of the country's power, identity, voice, and, in many ways, its right to exist, felt liberating. Relaxing even. We will have to finally figure out if we even deserve the right to be a nation, she thought. And, if yes, what kind of nation we will be. What exactly was the point of us? She remembered, vaguely, her ex-lover's rant one afternoon at Chez Marie's in Tabarre about Haiti's lifelong bout of existential indecision. We seemed incapable of choosing between philosophies, he said. Communism or capitalism? Social democracy or plain-vanilla democracy? Tourism-driven or manufacturing-driven job and economic growth? The Americans, like the French before them, want nothing more than to make those decisions for us. We resist their interference and rightly so, but come on, people, can we collectively take responsibility for a way forward that benefits everyone and stick to it?!

Like certain artists, Natasha Robert enjoyed swimming in tragedies and not comedies—after all, great pieces of art or song, to her, almost always evoked the pulpy thrill of heroic death followed by births and resurrections—so she was blissfully indifferent to the degree to which these questions scared the bejesus out of most folks. Stop the car! she said. The car stopped.

What now? Bobo said.

She got out and stood on the scorching earth. The wrecked National Palace stood mute in front of her. She gently touched the black metal fence surrounding it. Behind her, across Avenue de la Republique, was Place Pigeon, where an upside-down rusty red Chevy and its injured owner, unbeknownst to her, yearned for her. When she was a kid, she was, like many people, afraid to even touch the gate surrounding the National Palace of Haiti, for it protected a building of almost sacred importance and bottomless terror. The stories of bizarre crimes to occupy and hold the palace were legion and grim. And crazy, her husband would say after he'd had one drink too many. What were these fools hoping to get when they fought and killed so much to get this bureau? This?! The last time he had one of those drunken fits, the old man who had probably sold his soul to become president had lost his balance and fell face-first to the floor. Right in front of his grand oak desk, with its vintage pens and ten-year-old PC. When she tried to help her husband get back on his feet, he waved her off. No! he said, Let me crawl. Let my face and tongue suck the floor, let the parquet be the last thing to hold back my vomit. Let my busted lip sting and my blood stick to the floor. I lick shoes for a living, don't I? What difference will licking another unwanted thing make? It was a sad night. It was their honeymoon.

Outside the palace a few days after the quake, wounded people moaned at her feet. She cupped her hand over her brow to block the sun and see better. The palace was shattered; its dome severed off its body. Natasha struggled to make out the location of offices and rooms. She almost found it difficult to remember what the building had looked like when it was, well, palatial, fit and gleaming white. Tall, lordly, inscrutable. Memories of a relatively healthy and perky Port-au-Prince began to fade, she found, and fade quickly. The image of the National Palace as she left it the morning before the earthquake might as well be sepia-toned in her mind's eye. She could as well have been looking at the Sphinx in Giza. A sparrow, black and smooth, swooped down and perched himself casually on a ledge near where the west wing of the palace used to be. That's where Alain was, Natasha thought. Life attracts life, and the sparrow was the first animal she had seen since the earthquake. Surely it's a positive sign! Natasha took off in a sprint down Avenue de la Republic along the palace gate.

Excuse me, excuse me, she said to the men and women and children underfoot along the way. Madame! Madame! It was Bobo, chasing her. The run felt good. The air flooding Natasha's lungs filled her with joy. In motion, on a run, she felt purposeful, no longer a victim. The stale smell of death that had coated her was temporarily banished. A hand on the cement pillar at the corner to help her keep her balance, Natasha turned on rue St. Honoré. This normally shady and cool street was as forlorn as any street in Port-au-Prince, but the people were engaged in the hope business. Men and some women were trying to dig people out of the debris of fallen houses. Even from across the street, Natasha could hear survivors' cries for help and pleas about injuries. Cell phones rang everywhere, causing rescuers to stop and look and shake their heads when they realized the ringing was from another phone. Every phone on the street chimed and chimed, it seemed, because practically everyone with a cell phone had someone he knew buried alive with a cell phone somewhere in the city. And that person was calling and calling for help. How do you focus on rescuing a stranger or neighbor when a loved one or a friend is calling you for help so insistently? How could you, Natasha, go through so much trouble to try to find this one friend when you knew you had friends and distant relatives all over town whose well-being should concern you? Leave me alone, conscience, Natasha thought with a shrug to the singsong of dozens of cell phone ringtones while speed-walking on rue St. Honoré. She reached the back of the National Palace and discovered that the entrance she'd hoped to use to get through a secret passageway to where she left Alain was crushed beyond use. She covered her mouth.

No, she said, shaking her head. Not you. You can't be dead. No!

Her heart finally said, Perhaps he really is. Her spirit gave in. Hope in her spacious soul was blown out like a candle. Out of the corner of her eyes, she saw Bobo quickly put his gun away. He took Natasha gently by the shoulders and into his massive arms to guide her away from the fallen manse.

We can't stay around here too long, Bobo said. People might recognize you.

Natasha let herself be walked toward the car. She didn't try to stop or wipe the cold tears streaming down her cheeks. She couldn't stop their flow even if she'd wanted to. Alain, Alain, oh Alain. Natasha folded herself in the car. One last glance at the palace, then the Range Rover pulled away. In a country where tradition called for people to build elaborate pink-and-green or sky-blue minihouses in cemeteries to host their dead loved ones, she thought the National Palace had become a regal resting place for the man she loved, a too damned saddening event for her to appreciate its irony. Not yet anyway.

A fey noon sun was aloft and hot. Glistening four-by-four trucks were parked at various points around the Champ de Mars. The trucks ferried international humanitarians to ground zero to dispense aid. Some of the trucks were painted alarmingly ugly colors, like the school bus yellow of the truck with the word "Scientology" emblazoned on it in a large red script. Bobo found Avenue John Brown too congested. They turned left instead, soon skirting Place Pigeon and passing Le Capitol movie theater. Men waving fists of money came banging at their windows, startling Natasha out of her despondency. They're money changers, Bobo said. They want to sell gourdes for US dollars. Look, they think you're a foreigner. Bobo made that remark cheerily, like it was a compliment of some kind.

Soon they were in Fort National, Natasha's neighborhood. More accurately, the car drove through the canyon of rubble and dead bodies formerly known as Natasha's neighborhood, chilling the blood in her veins. Inconsolable since seeing the National Palace, Natasha was now suffocated by grief. The guys avoided her eyes. There wasn't just pain in Natasha's heart. There was an emptiness. She felt hollowed out. A great chilling vacuum where the warmth of hot blood used to be.

Mon Dieu! Bobo exclaimed a few minutes later. The car came to another abrupt halt, compelling Natasha to wipe the tears from her eyes and reluctantly brace herself. In front of them was the National Cathedral. Nôtre Dame de l'Assomption of Haiti, Natasha's favorite place in the whole world, loomed before them as a mix of rubble and jagged, broken concrete. Its towering pink and beige walls had been rent asunder by the earthquake. The colorful stained-glass windows Natasha spent almost a decade working on were shattered and scattered on the streets. The roof was sheared off the church's head, probably collapsed into the pews, smothering the altars and snuffing out remembrance candles. They stepped out of the SUV and walked on rue St. Laurent dazed, as if answering a mysterious call. The sky was electric blue. There was a small fire ablaze down the street. Piles of gray and pink cement had swallowed the front gate and sidewalk. Natasha could barely make out the top of the church's front door. But she badly needed to go inside. Giving up on the National Palace after the earthquake had split it in two and spread its interior on the ground like a spilled deck of cards was one thing. There was a former lover buried in that newly minted national tomb who deserved a better fate and proper mourning, like, she suspected, she would have to do for more than a few friends and former colleagues around town. But the thing between her and the cathedral was different. It was personal. It was about saving her sanity and, more important, her soul, the meaning of her life and afterlife.

Natasha was an old hand at grieving for loves lost. She had given up hope of having any surviving relatives in Haiti long before the earthquake. If they didn't come out of the woodwork to reach out to her after her name and face had made the news when she married the president of the freaking republic, they couldn't possibly exist anywhere on God's green earth. She really was the last of her kind on this *maudit* planet. This was why the sight of the Catholic cathedral, even gutted by Mother Nature, stiffened her spine. The church had had the effect of making Natasha feel . . . salvageable . . . ever since she was a child. And on this day, the church needed her to try to repair it and make it relevant again; maybe they could save each other. Natasha started climbing the rubble toward the door and thinking about the ways Jesus had been good to her via this cathedral. She was around ten years old the day the pack of boys chased her down rue Borgella. She deserved the ass-kicking coming to her. She had taken their soccer ball on an impulse during their game. They wanted the ball back, and they wanted to teach her the lesson to not mess with them in the process. Natasha's heart leapt in her chest, tickling her throat, but she outran the boys. Yes, she did. She took their ball for no reason as it rolled out of bounds, and ran away laughing. The boys screamed, cursed, and gave a chase that got more and more futile, so she smiled, relaxed. The air felt sweet, pumping her muscles to the point that she feared they might burst, explode. But she had relaxed a little too much in her sprint. One boy caught up to her and touched her shoulder. *Putain!* Natasha made a sharp turn to shake his grip, opened a gate and closed it, padlocking it. Give us the ball! Give us the ball! the boys bayed at the gates, arms outstretched. Natasha felt powerful, like Joan of Arc. When it seemed as though the boys' frustration would tear the gate apart, she giggled and tossed the ball over it. The ball flew into the sky, disappeared briefly in the white sun, then thudded on someone's face. The boys welcomed the ball like a long-lost friend and went back to playing their soccer match. Except for one of them. He lingered behind long enough to make sinister eye contact with Natasha. He gave her the I'll-slash-your-throat-for-that sign with his fingers. She gulped.

Well, that wasn't a smart thing to do, young lady, a deep voice intoned behind her.

Natasha turned to discover the voice belonged to the monsignor, Monsignor Dorélien. He stood over Natasha under the arch, between heavy metal doors. He looked like a young Desmond Tutu, darting eyes, smiling round face, big hands. Behind him a vast hall with a marbled cool beckoned. Natasha finally realized where she had escaped to. The National Cathedral. A building she didn't like much as a child, though she lived nearby. She couldn't remember the reason. Her parents, back when they lived together, forced her to go to Mass on Sundays. For some reason, after she became an orphan, she thought that if there was going to be one perk from that unwanted state, it would be the right to skip out of attending sermons about love every week. What time could she have for such nonsense after all her loves had disappeared or given her away? Uh-oh, she thought, looking at the monsignor. Young Natasha felt guilty for calling his work bullshit, even if it was only in her head.

Come in, child, he said. I know that boy. He'll be waiting for you for hours. You're welcome to wait him out here. Give him and his friends time to cool off.

This can't turn out good, Natasha thought. However, getting those boys to chase her into the church's protection turned out to be the single best mistake of her life. The cathedral Natasha walked into that day a decade ago was a *chantier* of artistic activity. High above the neat rows of brown wooden pews and the cream-white marble floors, which felt nice and cool under Natasha's naked feet, men and some women hung from all the church's stained-glass windows. They stood on scaffolding, to be sure. The paintbrushes they held caught Natasha's eyes. The workers had their backs turned away from the world. They were literally painting Jesus's grace onto the windows. The windows were high and long and skinny. The sun bathed them with approval, like God was thanking the artists for their work. Natasha had walked the aisles of the National Cathedral dozens of times before. Usually, she had been dragged against her will by a particularly religious prostitute friend who was going to take communion at Mass. During those trips down the aisle, Natasha looked down at the floor, partly out of respect for the grandeur of the moment of worship, but mostly out of embarrassment. She had never been baptized. Many of the worshippers in the church those Sundays knew her as the eccentric local orphan who had never been baptized and thus never had a first communion, and therefore did not belong in their company at Mass, the one moment where their eyes could watch God and feel that He was returning their gaze. Young Natasha, however, did not meet those disapproving glances because she felt them valid. She could not articulate why, but Natasha thought they were wrong. God's eyes smiled on her too. She lowered her eyes as a way to prove to the Lord that she could submit to at least one person's will—Jesus's—and to prove to herself that she was not some wild, untamable animal, no matter what people said. For a few minutes on the occasional Sunday, she, too, could get over herself and appreciate the cool smallness of submitting to the unknowable, endlessly vast presence of Jesus, his Father, and the Holy Ghost. The day Monsignor Dorélien invited her into the church in its off-hours Natasha looked up and around the cathedral for the first time. The place was huge! And rich with colorful mosaics and rainbow-colored stained-glass windows. Natasha felt the thrill of her id snap, crackle, pop, and for the first time she didn't feel guilty in the flow of artistic inspiration. The cathedral was not empty with a tomblike chill, as a big church on a weekday morning could be. Instead, the cathedral, to Natasha's eyes, seemed to be in the process of becoming, of being held up by the hands of two dozen artisans who were working at its various windows with fierce, happy concentration. They seemed to be transforming the National Cathedral into something worthy of heaven, or at least something inspiring to the eyes of parishioners seeking glimpses of heaven. To Natasha, the artists at work were doing the work she'd dreamed of doing, even when she didn't know how they did it. The artists were artisans, but they looked like conduits to God. She did not know you could be both.

That day, Monsignor Dorélien stood back to carefully observe the wonder in the little girl's eyes. The girl actually sat down in a pew to watch the stained-glass-window makers and cleaners work. She was entranced, like she was at the cinema. Oh, how Monsignor Dorélien longed to see some of the perpetually in motion children in the neighborhood pause to do just that. With a wave of an arm, the monsignor caught the attention of a glass maker.

Natasha watched the woman scamper down the scaffolding. The woman was a girl not much older than Natasha. She was short and wore no makeup, denim overalls, and the sauntering self-confidence that comes with a history of successfully deploying God-given gifts. With the glow of a thousand sunlit shards of rainbow-colored glass behind her, the woman said, Hi, I'm Vanessa. Then she shocked Natasha by shaking her hand, as if Natasha was her equal. Vanessa offered to show Natasha how to do what she did: make and paint church windows with scenes of biblical stories and figures.

Go ahead, Monsignor Dorélien said to Natasha. Vanessa's one of our brightest young painters. She'll show you the ropes, if you're interested. Young Natasha couldn't believe her luck.

Today, almost a decade and an earthquake later, in the roofless and almost window-free ruins of the cathedral, Natasha saw Monsignor Dorélien half-buried under chunks of church walls fallen on the exact spot where she'd met the woman who taught her how to paint and sculpt homages to God.

DAMAGED GOODS

In the refugee camp at Place Pigeon, Alain Destiné, Natasha's wounded ex-boyfriend, alternated between looking forward to death and mainlining nostalgia for her love, until one night his life was saved by a white man. The night had been so black and gloomy that the darkness muffled the crackle of Alain's fire. The camp had decided it needed a security force within days of its setting up a governing structure. No guns or knives were available, so a warm body armed with nothing more than a whistle would have to do. This night, it was Alain's turn to be the camp's night watchman. As the refugee camp in Place Pigeon had slowly morphed from a wreckage of the wrecked, terrified, and desperate to a loosely organized family of the wrecked, terrified, and desperate, small, interesting things had happened. The camp begat small plots of property, corridors with names, and a health clinic manned often by visiting foreigners and local student nurses and doctors, and also a restaurant, a church, a barbershop, a couple of beauty salons, a brothel, and even a small pharmacy and liquor store. Yes, the pharmacy and liquor store were one and the same. As they should be, Philippe said at the pharma-bar's opening. Philippe, God bless his heart, had even tracked down a pot dealer who made regular visits to the camp. Alain Destiné, who had been a model of dull and curmudgeonly sobriety all his life, evolved into a dull and curmudgeonly pothead after the earthquake. *If I had any talent for music I'd be on my way to becoming a Haitian Bob Marley right about now,* he wrote Natasha in his diary one afternoon.

The night Philippe told him it was his turn to play police chief of Place Pigeon's one-man police force, Alain went with the flow and assumed his responsibilities, as with everything in the passive existence he'd accepted after the earthquake. He accepted his turn in the rotation without protest in the name of solidarity with his ragtag group of new neighbors, even though he was one of the least physically able men or women in the refugee camp. Alain had a nonfunctioning leg with problems that had scared off visiting doctors. Malnutrition had left him without arm strength to swing a bat with any meaningful force, not that a baseball bat was available. (Christian, Philippe's new contact at an aid agency who worked in procurement, had yet to come up with one bat for the camp. Apparently, demand was high. No shit.) This night Alain was meant to sit outside his tent and listen to the radio to scare off potential burglars and malefactors with a display of vigilance, insomnia, and sentient life. Yes, some people actually burgled refugees' tents in Port-au-Prince after the disaster. Don't ask Alain why. It was one of so-called God's many fucking jokes. Ha-ha, very funny, motherfucker. There was nothing of value left to steal among these invalids, except people's last shred of dignity and courage. Those commodities were at their lowest ebb. Haitians found facing the future to be exquisitely diffi-cult after the most reliable thing they had ever known in their lives, the ground they stood on, had decided to violently betray them without warning. When it came to the thieves, Alain was actually forgiving. I guess some people clearly have habits that were hard to break even after an apocalypse, he thought. Even in hell those people will be around, looking to cut corners, Natasha would add if she had been by his side, sitting on the dirt, head on his shoulders while listening to his trembling whine and staring at the firelight. Alain tried not to think about Natasha too often. It was too disabling. The emotions her name generated in his heart were hot and ranged from desperate yearning to rage. His memories of Natasha were wonderful and dangerous and thus a distraction, a lux-ury he couldn't avoid in the leadership thrust upon him by fate after the disaster. Besides, his love for her lacked purity. Purity was a new word to him. Even in business, Alain was never a numbers man. He was man of nuances, not blacks and whites. Shades of gray. Everyone and every problem was negotiable. And for what? What were you looking for back then, Alain? What returns on investment were so good that you channeled so much of your energy for them? What was the point of you?

Alain sighed, defeated by the presence of silence instead of answers. In fact, his head now hurt whenever he tried to think hard. Tea. He could use a cup of tea. With lots of milk and lots of honey. What's that sound? Straight ahead and walking toward Alain were four men, two in each alley of tents. They were poking their heads in and out of tents of sleeping refugees. They were the land pirates of Port-au-Prince, and they had appeared out of thin air, like boogeymen, looking for bounty. The men were cloaked in darkness and they did their thieving with the assurance of soldiers wearing night-vision goggles in a desert. The whistle. Alain was supposed to whistle loud and high the minute he spotted intruders. The hope was the alarm would scare them into leaving the camp. In fear of what? As far as anyone could tell, the meager Haitian National Police had disappeared in the earthquake. The United Nations soldiers were there to work on their tans and protect shady political manipulations and not protect the lives of common men. Where the hell was that whistle? Alain patted the ground around him ever more frantically for a whistle that was actually tied around his neck. He knocked over a can. The fire shuddered.

The thieves turned toward Alain as one. They saw Alain and Alain saw them. Their leader, tall and light-

skinned with feral teeth and a half-afro—a half-fro—
walked quickly toward Alain, an index finger over his lips
to order the crippled security volunteer to be quiet. Without breaking his stride, the man pulled a baseball bat from
behind his back and proceeded to prepare to go Reg-
gie Jackson on Alain's head. It all happened fast, too fast
for Alain to even think about screaming for help. Arms
crossed over his face, Alain braced for the coming thump
and the cracking of his skull . . . and death, yes, fresh-ass
death. Darkness, his new friend. Alain put his arms down
and turned his chin up toward the fast-coming fat end of
the baseball bat. Then Alain heard a crunch, but felt nothing but the spray of a liquid across his face. He opened his
eyes and saw a man, a white man, whack another marauder
with a backswing of a baseball bat. What the fuck? Alain
thought, How come everyone in this town has a baseball
bat except me? The foreigner was clearly deft with a bat,
so the last two thieves decided to abort their mission and
sprinted out of the camp, damn near impaling themselves
while jumping over its pale green fence before disappearing into the night. Alain's unexpected savior watched
them scamper with a faint smile of satisfaction on his face.
It was a familiar face, lined and expressive even in repose.
A dimpled chin, a forest of malleable hair. The man was
handsome. Movie-star handsome.

Are you OK, buddy? he said.

Wait, he *is* a movie star, Alain realized, though he
couldn't place the man's most famous film. Something in

the eighties. It was the reassuring twinkle of the man's eye that gave it away. When Alain was in graduate school in Greenwich Village, Hollywood stars were commonplace in the neighborhood. Buying records at Tower, lunching at the coffee shop, even buying weed in Washington Square Park. The girls were occasionally seducible. The men were unapproachable. They all had that twinkle at the ready, though. It functioned like a shield and a dagger of otherworldly charm. Successful politicians and CEOs have a variation of it. Musicians too. The theatrical variation was a tad more delicate and effervescent, which is maybe why it had a longer-lasting effect on most mortals.

What the hell are you doing here? Alain said. I was doing fine.

You were? Really? What was that hands-down, chin-up move? Some form of Haitian jujitsu?

Fuck off.

Naw, I'm too tired from saving your ass.

The guy plopped down on the patch of brown grass next to Alain's tent. His chest heaved. He was clearly exhausted. Obviously, playing hero against hungry thieves in a park in the middle of the Caribbean night with a baseball bat was not a routine night out for him. He looked to be around fifty, fit, for sure, but gray at the temples. Wiry and lean, probably vegan, all the veins in his bright pink face and arms popped out, throbbing. His heart was probably playing a tambourine in his chest. In front of them, the two marauders lay unconscious, lifeless.

Hollywood, as Alain dubbed the white man in his head, avoided looking at them, as if he felt distaste for the violence he'd just practiced. Alain looked at them. Under the light of a piercing silver moon, their lifeless faces made them look younger than he'd expected. Their clothes were threadbare. Their faces just plain bare. Maybe they were just hungry and couldn't sleep and were looking for help. Maybe they weren't the leaders at all, just frontline pawns now nursing frontal lobe fractures. Either way they had gone about looking for help the wrong way. The poor bastards. Why they had come out here looking for trouble? In a couple of hours, the first Place Pigeon residents would wake up and see their bodies and feel as though they had come face to face with loups-garous, werewolves, the monsters of the night featured in Haitian bedtime stories. These two boys would serve as a deep reminder about how screwed up and scary people could still be, not just the traitorous earth.

We have to move their bodies, Alain said without taking his eyes off them.

Yeah, Hollywood said.

Hollywood went to work. Under Alain's jealous eyes, the man from the city of pretend heroes solemnly picked up and dragged each dead stranger's body with the help only of the bright moonlight over to the camp's cemetery, then dug a hole and buried them. Alain saw the foreigner tenderly bury his dead compatriots with disbelieving eyes and pangs of guilt from his inability to help. The graves were crude, not that deep. The dirt covering them was thin. A good gust of prehurricane wind in the summer could unmask the dead and their seemingly slumbering faces. People around the world tended to presume the dead were innocent, or that each death, with its complete finality, deserved our pity, even sympathy, because a dead bastard, even though he was a bastard, is, after all, still dead, dealing with the great unknowns of fate, reinforcing our core belief that no one deserves to die, especially us. There had to be something self-serving in this view, Alain had come to think. It must mean that if one accepts that some or most people deserve to die—since until God tells us otherwise, everyone will die, and deservedly so, as far as He seems concerned—the implication is that I deserve to die too, and this idea sucks too much for a lot of people to accept. No one wants to die. Even people who believe in heaven don't want to die. Even the elderly, reduced to infantilism and practically mute, stunned with constant pain, always feel death is a dish that will be best served to their friends and not them, because, well, they are special, and their friends clearly less special and more deserving to die than they are, though they love their friends and wish them heaven. Those on their deathbeds are probably not unlike most of us in that way too. They believe deep in their bones that a last-minute escape from death will materialize and protect them when they need it most, when death comes calling, whether they expected her or not, and whether they believed they earned heaven or hell.

Alain stopped being one of those people after the earthquake. The second after he woke up on the dirt from the earth's blow, and for the many days afterward that he spent helplessly watching piles of extinguished human bodies grow and grow around him and be removed from sight like so much trash, he couldn't for the life of him figure out why he deserved to live and so many people deserved to die during and after those fateful thirty-five seconds. The numbers of dead from the earthquake and aftershocks were estimated to range from a few thousand to a million, according to news reports on Radio Ginen. Knowing full well that the correct number would fall somewhere in the middle, about a half million, if Haiti was lucky, Alain found the blow to his society to be particularly grotesque. He couldn't find the optimistic muscles to forgive God. He couldn't question God's sanity candidly, even to himself, so he did what so many people do when convulsed by divine deception: he put his own faith in question. He wondered whether he deserved another dawn, another dream, more human touch. He found himself wanting. His impulse was to negate his own existence. He accepted a growing belief that life was fleeting and trivial and death could be a respite, and even a reward, from it all. Though the presence of strange little Xavier occasionally pacified his spiritual torment, when the boy slept, Alain felt the misery in the people around him and across the island fall over his head, against his will, like an assault of a thousand jackhammers. He'd sit on his cardboard cushion and stare at his stretched-out wounded leg and zone out. Anything was better than sleep and the recurring nightmare of an avalanche of crippled and dead Haitians asking him, Why? Why? Why? WHY? as he ran away. They were always in a fucking forest. Running and running and running, breathlessly. The dead kept chasing Alain from all angles. Their questions were louder each time. Why? Why? WHY? I don't know! I don't know! I don't know! Alain screamed while running for his life.

That's pretty good use of the word "fuck," Hollywood said, ending Alain's reverie.

The movie star had plopped down on the ground next to him. Thoroughly exhausted, he looked at least fifty years old, about twice Alain's age. His face was heavily lined and pink and crinkly-eyed handsome. He radiated warmth, not grandiosity, probably to protect Alain's ego, probably out of habit. He unpacked his duffel bag and seemed to need to connect with Alain to work through the adrenaline high of his extraordinary efforts that evening.

I think I recognize your accent, he said. Brooklyn, right? You're a New Yorker.

Yeah, Alain said. Some of the time.

I was born there. Parents moved us to California not long after.

I was born here, Alain said, and moved out there soon afterward. California's nice. Good weather.

Not as nice as the weather here.

You like it here, huh?

What's not to like? The weather, the women, the music, the art, the food, the dancing, the women, the women. Did I mention the women? I could be very happy here. Say, that leg looks fucked-up. Have you had someone look at it?

Yeah, then they looked away.

Funny. Get some rest. I'll be awake for another couple of hours.

No, man, you should get some sleep. You had a heck of a night. Just leave that bat with me.

I'd love to, but I can't sleep. I haven't been able to sleep since I saw the first CNN report on the earthquake. People running, crying, buildings falling, confused children. When I close my eyes and relax, I see them chasing me.

Me too.

Same dream?

Same nightmare.

Why don't you go home? You sound like someone who probably has a nice home in the hills here. You know they were largely untouched right?

I'm not surprised. God protects the rich.

Look, God had nothing to do with what happened here.

Was that supposed to make me feel better?

You know what I mean.

Why don't you go home? You have no business here.

In the black of the night, they heard a stirring. A crunch. It was creepy. Really, couldn't the earthquake have left at least one functional streetlight? Alain thought. Alain and Hollywood tensed up and tried to play it cool at the same time. The noise came from behind where they were sitting. New marauders were in Alain's tent. Fuck. A hand touched Alain's shoulder from the side. It was Xavier. Only he could sneak up and touch you without scaring the shit out of you. How the hell does he do that?

Xav, *c'est toi*! Alain said.

The six-year-old newly minted orphan nodded in a way that told Alain it was OK for him to breathe easy. He was in good hands.

Meet our new neighbor . . .

Steve.

Hollywood's real name was Steve, but Alain preferred calling him Hollywood, as he watched hands that had held Oscars shake Xavier's hand. Xavier held the star's hands in both of his and looked at the scars on Hollywood's wrists. Hollywood turned red with shame. Hollywood looked away.

Nice to meet you, little guy, he said. I'm going to get some rest now. It's been a long night.

With that, Hollywood crawled into the little tent he had pitched and promptly fell asleep. His Timberland boots poked outside it. Xavier looked at Alain and suggested he do the same. Alain dragged himself into their tarp tent and promptly fell asleep too, despite the crowing of roosters and the azuring sky outside.

Alain Destiné did not dream that evening, nor did he have time to write a diary entry to Natasha about the movie star who saved his life. In fact he didn't get to sleep much at all before a commotion outside his tent woke him up. He heard a happy voice, that of Philippe, his comrade in refugee leadership, calling his name.

Alain! Alain! You got to hear this!

Alain rolled over and began to crawl out of his tent. His upper-body strength had improved enough that his face no longer grazed the mud in his tent when he crawled out of it. Once his face had appeared outside the tent, Philippe and another buddy, Gilbert, gave him a hand to get on his feet. Shading his eyes from the bright sun, he saw Hollywood sitting on the ground outside his tent, sipping a cup of coffee, casually, so cool in fact he might as well have been in Saint-Tropez or Saint Bart's instead of disaster-struck Port-au-Prince. Beyond Philippe's entourage, a crowd of refugees were coming toward Alain's tent, no doubt to hear what the commotion was about too.

Man, listen to her, Philippe said. Her idea is genius! Genius.

A bright, freckle-faced little girl of about twelve years old emerged from the middle of the crowd. In that typically Haitian way of talking, as if addressing a nation after a march on Washington, she said her name was Alyssa. Mr. Alain, she said, I think the camp could use a memorial in honor of the people who died during the earthquake.

A what?

A memorial, sir. A piece of architecture, art, or a quiet area where, if you see it, you are meant to pause in tribute to all the lives we lost and be grateful and optimistic about the future. I had an uncle who visited from New York after 9/11, and he said just reading about people arguing about what shape the memorial should take helped New Yorkers begin to recover from the 9/11 terrorist attacks. I think trying to put a memorial in Place Pigeon would do the same for people here.

What the fuck is this little girl talking about? Alain thought. To Alain, a moment of pause during these stressful times had come to mean time for reflection, and reflection meant time to cut yourself with soul-searing grief about the past events and the vagaries of the future, which was inevitably transformed into volcanic anger at the intolerably sunny but unknowable future of their people. "Our" people, that is the key word, isn't it? Chill out, Alain. The girl might be on to something.

Think about it, Alain, Philippe said. If Place Pigeon becomes the first refugee camp to establish a memorial for those suffering from goudou-goudou, we'll get more attention than the other camps, and more help. The world will know we're ready to work our way out of this mess.

We have to do it. Especially considering our location across from the Palais. Look how fucked-up it still is!

Alain didn't look. He avoided looking at it these days. Too disheartening.

And, if you pull it off, you'll show the world that Haitians can take care of and honor themselves, Hollywood said.

These were his first words to anyone other than Alain since he'd installed himself in Place Pigeon. Everyone turned their attention en masse to the blue-eyed man in their midst. It was as if they hadn't noticed he was there all that time. So he can talk, an old lady on Alain's right said.

As you guys can tell, I'm not from here. *Mon français est très moche*, Steve said.

Haitians don't say *moche*, Alain thought. The French do. But everyone got the gist of what Hollywood was trying to say anyway.

Where I come from, and around the world, everyone feels terrible about what happened to you. The damage the earthquake caused is horrible. It's mind-blowing, really. In fact, because we sense how great your need is, my people also know that whatever help we send you will only scratch the surface. It'll barely make a dent. We'll barely stop the bleeding. But that's OK. Yes, it is, really. You guys have taken care of yourselves for centuries. Before the white men came. Even before the Africans came. This place is never going to be Switzerland. It never was, nor does it aspire to be, right? But you manage. You make the best of things anyway, don't you?

A few uh-huhs floated through the crowd. Not bad, Hollywood. Alain thought. I might have to rename you Oscar. Go on.

I'm pretty useless to your deep humanitarian needs. They're out of my league. I'm rich, but I ain't that rich.

A few people chuckled.

I'm here because I need redemption, Hollywood said. I need to work for you and for you to eventually tell me I'm an OK human being. My second wife left me last fall after twenty years of putting up with my dickhead ways. No one wants to talk to me where I live. Everyone took her side. And rightly so. Only my agent takes my calls these days.

C'est quoi ça?

It was a teenager. He, like most of them, had no idea what an agent was. Get it together, Hollywood Alain thought. You might lose them.

An agent? An agent is your best friend in the world as long as your work gets them a percentage of your income so that they can enjoy it more than you. Anyway, my work is not that important. I'm not a doctor or an alchemist or Rambo. All of whom would be far more useful to you in the situation you live in these days than an actor.

Ah-ha, Alain thought. You really are that movie star! Shit, what was your best movie? The one when you played the rapist? Or the cokehead or the corrupt cop? Come to think of it, you're damn good at playing creeps. No wonder you can't keep your women.

Good for nothing as I am, I think I can help you put together a great memorial. After all, spectacle is my forte. You guys are pretty ahead of the curve by thinking of this project this soon during the crisis. I think it's a terrific idea.

All right then, Alain said. Thank you. Everybody, this is Steve. Thanks also for choosing to help our community, Steve. We know you could be anywhere in the world but here. We're grateful for that. So . . . what's your name again?

Alyssa, said the girl.

Alyssa, do you have a particular type of memorial in mind? Across the Champ de Mars, there already exists a hideous tower bequeathed to us by an otherwise smart past president. Our memorial has to have two phases: one we could set up a quick and interesting foundation for in the short term, and another for long-term construction.

I don't know, Alyssa said. I like statues.

Good idea, Alain said. We all like statues, I think. Is there a sculptor around?

How about a beam of light like New York City did on the site of the twin towers? a boy named Gilbert said.

How about fireworks? another kid said.

Oy vey, Alain thought. This is going to take a while.

No, no, we should create something using the cheapest and most available material around us, a busty woman said.

Like what? Gilbert said. Mud?

Well, yes, the woman said.

Man, she had canons, Alain thought. Sweat from the scalding midday heat drenched them. They glistened. We should build a statue as a tribute to them, Alain thought. You could hold an entire nation happily aloft on them shits.

Mud! Hollywood said, snapping his fingers. That's a great idea! I once saw a piece, I don't remember where, Art Basel Miami or in Basel. It was a giant swan made of mud. It was great, soaring even. Very inspiring. It looked like chocolate and did not fall apart at all. Show of hands: Who can sculpt? A dozen hands went up.

Really? Alain thought. That many of y'all can sculpt? Jesus, you people are so easy to underestimate.

Good, good, Hollywood said. He was excited. Hey—Philippe, is it? Why don't you lead our little team of sculptors and visionaries on a walk around the park, so we can find a suitable location for the memorial?

If I may, I would suggest you explore a location somewhere along the fence facing Avenue de la République. It's the street with the most traffic, thus the memorial would get the most attention.

Good idea! Hollywood said, as if genuinely surprised Alain could have one of those or care enough to share it.

The idea of a memorial, a thing that would honor their dead and express their collective vision and hope for their future, a concept heretofore alien and even absurd to the most ardent dreamers among them, energized the small community of walking wounded survivors in Place Pigeon like nothing else, not even the occasional food distribution by the United Nations. Even Alain was swept up in the moment and the emotion and visions of that heart-pumping thing called a future, a better tomorrow. Buoyed, he stood on his crutches and watched Alyssa and Philippe and Steve's merry band walk off to peruse the camp's perimeter under the cheer of passing doves and golden sunlight. A place to plant their symbol of the future! Who'da thunk it! A future. We could have one. We were entitled to one. Ah, from the mouth of babes. The fresh wave of positive thinking of a future made of ideas of community, peace, and love and cheer, and not just plentiful food and medicine and schools and life in a city without debris had a cooling effect on Alain, wiping away the sweat on his brow and dramatically increasing his sense of fellowship with his fellow men and women. Around him everyone felt that way. They were all thinking the same thing: What will our future look like? What should our future look like? The only way forward from here was up. Had to be.

His hand began to tremble. His body was tired from holding him up with crutches. Pain made his foot throb. His vision blurred. Mr. Alain? said Raymonde, one of the camp's sages. She spoke rarely, but her big, booming presence was never ignored. Mr. Alain, why don't let me do something about that leg? I know a potion that could help.

Yes, OK. Anything, Alain said. Anything to stop the pain.

He let himself fall in Raymonde's meaty open arms, fainting. Raymonde caught him as if he were a child who weighed no heavier than a feather.

A little-known fact was that the president of Haiti was secretly a Madonna fan. A huge one. When alone in his office in the National Palace of Haiti during moments of high tension, he'd press play on the greatest-hits album, *The Immaculate Collection*, an inexplicable but surprisingly wonderful birthday gift from a US ambassador. Every line in the fourth song, "Like A Virgin," gave him immeasurable pleasure. At the 1:38 mark, when the Material Girl went *heee* in the chorus, the old man felt all the pressure seep out of his shoulders. His whole body exhaled. His stresses, ecstatically albeit all too briefly, were replaced with the lightness of being that was generally associated with the smiles of children at play in grassy parks on summer days. Despite his efforts at discretion, the President's infatuation with the tart from Michigan was well known among the cabinet. Now the cabinet was dead. Each member reduced to dust by the quake. The

President hadn't had access to Madonna in the intervening weeks. He craved her. There had been no balm for the
Herculean strength he summoned to give his wounded
country the look of having a pulse. In the aftermath of the
earthquake's carnage, he walked the streets, collar open,
shoes dusty, and hugged everyone in sight. Be it strangers
or friends, it didn't matter. He couldn't tell the difference anymore. Everyone knew him; no one asked him
how he felt. On crowded street corners under a brilliant
sun or a maudlin moon, he took in their grief. It was
the least he thought he could do. He listened patiently
to the painstaking details of their stories. He liked how
their voices went from high and hysterical to low and
soft after they discovered they had his undivided attention. The president of Haiti allowed himself to imagine
the horror of the circumstances of each individual's loss,
which invariably involved watching walls of houses and
buildings fall on themselves, lovers, parents, or children.
Or having a house or building or a lover, parent, or child
suddenly vanish without a trace during or after goudou-
goudou. Throughout these tours, he was there, but he was
not there. No one ever asked him how he experienced
goudou-goudou. It was as if no one noticed him as flesh
and blood and human. He had become an avatar, and he
himself began to notice his existence less and less too.

Mercifully, there was no rage yet in the country. Just
shock. Not "what the fuck" type shock, but a "why me"
type shock. Not self-pity, but an overwhelming sense of

pitifulness descended upon Haiti. Its hills, its trees, even its clouds, hung their heads low. Life was going to go on, but a feeling that it had deeply stalled overwhelmed everyone, and not just in Port-au-Prince, where the disaster had struck, but in peaceful and generally pristine communities as far from ground zero as Chambellan and Fort Liberté. It's not bad luck, Haitians had always figured. Life was just hard, absurdly so. They took comfort in knowing that life abroad was not anxiety-free either. Life was supposed to be hard, for us to appreciate its stretches of sweetness. If you expected life to be easy, you were an idiot. But this new blow was too brief, sudden, and violent. It would take a long time to get used to.

Of course, the world did not allow Haiti to lick its wounds in solitude. Once the initial wave of sympathy and pledges of support had died down, some people began looking for ways to find the president of Haiti wanting. Most Haitians were still looking for what hit them, but some folks needed to hit something. They needed a scapegoat. It's natural. When you can't blame God or his girlfriend, Mother Nature, or you can blame them but get little satisfaction from holding a grudge against our invisible overlords, it makes much more sense to look askance at the head of state. The young aide who was telling the President all this in the limo trudging toward Manhattan spoke like it was news. He wore a dark suit, a blue shirt, and a dark tie that were all one size too big. He spoke in a whisper, as though he were delivering the Word to the old man. All in an effort to appear calm and reassuring and to becalm and reassure a president he assumed had to be freaked out of his mind. They were in the back of a limousine in New York City a month after the quake. They were about to meet a gaggle of the President's peers, people the kid assumed would look down on the President even as they pressed mounds of cash into his hands to help Haiti's reconstruction, per the orders of their truly dismayed citizenry.

New York City made the President think of no one else but Madonna. He disliked the Big Apple, but the city had given the world Madonna, an angel if there ever was such a thing. It couldn't be all bad. The President's arrival at JFK Airport that wintry afternoon had been rocky. An airline stewardess actually took his freshly buttered bread out of his hand right before he could bite into it because the plane was about to land. He never felt rage hotter than the one he felt looking at the prim and prissy bitch standing over him in the airplane. He glared hard. His bodyguards and new aides had to drag and push the old man off the plane and through customs. The President was so mad he didn't bother closing his coat in the face of the first blast of cold winds that greeted them outside JFK. In silence, they walked toward a black town car whose chauffeur had smartly, though rudely, decided not to leave the driver's seat to brave the elements and open the door for the visiting head of state he was there to pick up. Of course, there was a snowstorm. It's rare that snowstorms don't greet you when you visit New York City from tropical Port-au-Prince in February, the President thought, a truism he first experienced in his twenties. Ice daggers rained from the gray sky. The air was still and quiet, yet rough and menacing. The brick buildings of Queens's rows of warehouses looked bombed-out in the stormy haze. It was morning, but dark like dusk. The President's group heard icicles whistle through the air, searching for exposed skin to prick and cut open. In the car, the President soon realized the thing making the incessant buzzing sound he had been hearing was in his pocket. He fumbled a bit with the new device, a BlackBerry, then watched a message from Bobo unfurl.

We found Destiné, boss. I sent a few of the boys for him. He was in a refugee camp where he is living for no apparent reason. They went there in the afternoon. No guns. I gave them baseball bats to protect themselves. It can get wild in those camps sometimes. They say the place was filthy and crowded. I told them to be nice and discreet. Destiné seemed to have been living there since the quake, they said. They said he was hurt, a broken leg. Either way he had no intention of leaving the camp to go to the hospital or just go home. Could be he's gone crazy. There's a lot of that happening since goudou-goudou. We didn't expect any trouble. But the guys told me that as soon as they approached his tent in the camp, twenty guys with guns showed up. If it's true, boss—and we have no reason not to trust these guys; they're pros; I've used them before—if it's true, I think Destiné might be raising a militia to come after you. His security guards killed two of our guys. The two others barely got away safely. They said Destiné's guards had big guns. Maybe Destiné's fallen in with Colombian drug runners? He's pretty shifty. According to the guy I have watching him 24 hours a day, Destiné is now friends with some famous American actor. They have even appeared on TV. They're building a memorial to the victims of goudou-goudou made of mud in Place Pigeon. The international press loves them. Reporters and camera crews are always over there, swarming them. It's complicated but we'll keep trying to get him. You can count on me, boss!

Don't worry about your wife, sir. We have her under constant surveillance too. You're right. She's a good girl. She's never left the Cathedral. I have a guy bring her food and supplies daily. She's taking care of Monsignor Dorélien, who's near death. She stopped going out, and she seems to have forgotten about looking for Destiné.

Faithfully yours, Bobo.

The President wanted to slam the device against the wall or break it apart with his hands, but this was the wrong time for him to show any signs of weakness. The mood in the car, which was now rumbling along the Fifty-Ninth

Street bridge, was tense enough. The members of his government's new makeshift cabinet were heading into the biggest negotiations of their lives. They were young and not eager to find out just how deeply unprepared for the moment they were.

Bobo was lying, the President thought. Bobo had always been a lousy liar. That's the main reason the President had trusted him over so many others throughout the years. Somewhere in Bobo's bumbling dissembling was the nugget of information the President needed to make his next decision. Bobo's idiots for hire probably did indeed find Destiné and fail to get him. But they didn't fail because Destiné had assembled a revolutionary army of *sans abris* to scare them. Destiné was a smart kid who was capable of many things, but at his core he was a loner, a talker and not a fighter. It was the character flaw that prevented him from becoming a leader of men in the best of times in Haiti. These were not the best of times in Haiti. Did Destiné talk his way out of capture? Possibly. The kid was magnetic, and, boy, could he talk a good game. Why didn't he have the decency of doing me a favor and die already?

At this thought, the President saw his conscience take the form of his predecessor Métélus with big old white angel wings. What are you doing, man? You never hurt anyone intentionally in your life.

And what of it? the President said.

You knew Bobo would misinterpret your request that he find Destiné for you. You just wanted the kid found by your people before your wife did. You hoped they found his body, deceased. Of all the Haitians the earthquake killed, surely, *ce merde de Destiné* would have been one of them, right? That was too much to hope for, old friend. Destiné is your cross to bear.

The man is fucking my wife, the President said.

You don't know that for sure.

The President gave the angel a blank stare.

OK. He's fucking your wife.

I got other crosses to bear.

Like, what? Leading a ruined country with few resources?

Yes, that.

That's easy, man. That's playing with house money. You know that. Heads you win. Tail you win.

Mais, compère, the kid is fucking your wife! the devil said, waving a pitchfork on the President's left shoulder. He looked a lot like Duvalier *le père*.

You've been a good boy all your life. You're entitled to snuffing out one life with your presidential privilege before you leave office, especially after all the horrors you've been through with the earthquake and all. *Écoute*, he was fucking your wife in your own palace! What the fuck's the point of working your whole life to become master of your own palace when young bastards are going to stroll through the front door to sleep with your woman? He fucked her well too. Real good. If he's crippled from the earthquake, you'll be putting him out of his misery.

Besides, it's not like you're sending Navy SEALs on the other side of the planet to execute some son of a bitch you never met and calling it justice. Unlike that case, there are no courts of law, local or international, where you could bring charges of crimes against humanity against the kid. There isn't. No one will notice or mourn the boy's death, not even your old lady from the sounds of it. Isn't this what it's all about anyway? Her love. After removing the small hindrance of a typically over-reaching boy out of your marital lives, you'll have your lady all to yourself. Think about it, you'll be killing the boy for the love of a wonderful woman. How romantic is that? Isn't that His way? Shit, I should become a poet. Call me Cupid.

Don't listen to our predecessor over there, Mr. President, Métélus the angel said. You have a nice track record of resisting the impulse to abuse your privileges. There are many, many diplomatic and decent ways to deal with your issues with Alain Destiné. You know them well, instinctively. They will serve your purposes.

Thank you, gentlemen, the President said, blinking away the avatars of his good and evil instincts. I'll take it from here.

The President held off replying to Bobo's message with new orders.

The town car pulled in front of the United Nations headquarters, 405 East Forty-Second Street. Dark, cold clouds surrounded the tower of the Le Corbusier-designed Secretariat. The grandiosity of New York City generally made the President feel small. Tall buildings, seemingly held up by puffy clouds, that were lithesome in the summer and moody in the winters. Boroughs connected by long, winding, and lanky multilane bridges choked with giant delivery trucks whose rumbling sounds were always menacing and angry, like warnings to stay out of Gotham or to enter Gotham at your own peril. As the car made its way into the city, the President noted how easily people disappeared in New York City. In his decades of coming here, he couldn't say he'd actually seen a New Yorker in the same way that, for example, a visitor can see every bead of sweat, sinewy muscle, and concern in the face and body of a Haitian in his or her thin dress under the clinically unforgiving glare of the Caribbean sun. If the President saw New Yorkers at all, they were usually hidden in plain sight, walking fast, talking as if distracted, camouflaged by layers of clothing and hats and behind sunglasses and faraway stares no matter the season.

Chills ran up the President's spine to the back of his head from the tips of his toes. He had stepped into a puddle as he climbed out of the car. *Merde*, he said. Wet feet felt squishy. Guards in the lobby of the UN building greeted them with friendliness once the group emerged through revolving doors. A lassitude came over the President, and he walked with a stoop while entering an elevator. The kid on his right, his new foreign minister, stopped briefing the President on the agenda of the coming Conference to Take Over and Carve Up Haiti Further with the People Who Screw the World for the first time since they'd met in the new all-tent presidential quarters near Toussaint Louverture Airport. Finally! the President thought. He shut up. The elevator went up slowly. A hush fell over all of them. All eyes lifted toward the lights above, tracking their rise through floors with soft beeps. Most buildings in New York City did not have a thirteenth floor out of deference to some age-old superstition. But this building did, and it was off-limits to everyone except heads of states. Leaving his staff in the elevator, the President was greeted by a sumptuous dark red carpet and the biggest chandelier he had ever seen. A valet solemnly took his coat. The valet was also known as the secretary general of the United Nations. The man also known as the SG grasped the president of Haiti's hands and bowed. The President felt as if he were attending his own funeral.

So good to see you, Mr. President, the SG said. He was a slight man of indeterminate race with the honeyed voice of a practiced undertaker. I wish we were seeing each other under more cheerful circumstances.

I know, the President lied.

Come, the oily secretary general said, the others await. They are eager to share their sympathies with you.

Into the inner sanctum of the masters of planet earth, the President entered. He liked this part, a little. He liked how staff, ministers, generals, and business partners, not to say the media, were banned from getting off the elevator on this floor. A few years ago, the President had met the president of Benin on his way out. He had walked funny. What rotten luck could have happened to his country to force him to submit to such a gangbang?

My son, the president of Benin said to the president of Haïti, arms open. The Beninois's face actually went from bloodshot to something akin to a smile. The hug was heartfelt.

Oh, you didn't know Haitians were the sons of Benin? Where do you think your voodoo came from? Don't you know where Toussaint Louverture and his gang of rebel slaves were born? Oh, your stock's been watered down through the centuries, but look at you, handsome and proud. Those and all your other blessings came from Benin, my friend.

The President wasn't sure if this cheery African was lying or telling the truth, but during his embrace was the only time in his trips abroad the President had not felt like the loneliest man in the world.

The gang was all there when the President walked into the oak-paneled conference room. They wore dark suits and red or blue ties. The Frenchman was short. The German was tall. The Italian looked bored, and the Russian radiated sympathy. The Chinese was cool in thick black-frame glasses. The American was the only one sitting in a gold-trimmed armchair and smiling. He motioned for the Haitian to join him in a nearby chair. A glass of a well-cubed, dark and lovely drink materialized in the President's right hand. He sighed and sat down.

Look, man, the American said. That earthquake was fucked-up. I'm sorry. We're all sorry. How are things down there?

Bad, he said.

Katrina bad?

Hiroshima bad.

Goddamn it, the American said, slapping his thigh. That's fucked-up. I'm sorry to hear that, man. I really am. Why do bad things keep happening to the noble while the craven and feckless mint money without trying? Damn, that was good. I should write that down so I don't forget it. Dominic, write that down for me somewhere, will you? And text it to Anthony in Washington. Now where was I? Hiroshima bad, huh? That sounds expensive.

Yes, very.

We're willing to take care of you. We're humanitarians after all. We'll need a few things in return.

I know. But no more drugs, man. The people can't take any more pain.

Shh, shhh, the president of the US of A said. Don't worry about the details. You personally will be taken care of. The Tuscany deal still stands.

The American looked at his Italian counterpart. He nodded sagely.

But I have to go back . . .

Because your lady's still down there. We know. We're

all family men. You get home and get her. You get to stay until after the elections for your replacement. I think we'll schedule them for November. What do you think, fellas? November sounds like a good time?

The Haitian president's mind briefly checked out of the meeting with his grinning northern counterpart and his amigos.

Alain Destiné, his wife's friend, had been born under a lucky star. That's why the President had mixed feelings about him. A big part of him liked the kid. At age nine, when Alain's father, a colleague of the President's at medical school, had brought him to Haiti from abroad, the boy was beautiful, bright, curious, and tough in a way that made the President wish the boy was the son he suspected he would never have. As the years went on, he kept expecting the kid to grow out of that winner's sheen, especially after his father lost his prestigious job and retreated to the placid life of a bookstore owner on Place Boyer.

Instead, the boy grew bolder as he grew older. Destiné went from having a vitality the President admired to one the President envied. The boy lived like he expected to win—at soccer, at politics, at business, at love. The President, he played the angles and tried to come out ahead of losses, which had worked out reasonably well for him. The President dreamed of avoiding nightmares; Destiné seemed to dream mostly of glory. But Destiné overreached, didn't he? He overplayed his hand. You don't sleep with another man's wife. You certainly shouldn't

sleep with a friend and mentor's wife. No man is so stupid
not to know when his wife's fucking another man. No old
man anyway. Figuring out who the man is can be tricky.
But we become aware of it on some level the moment of
the first spark of electricity, the first penetration. *Pfft.* The
boy was his father's son. His father over-reached with the
wrong woman too, and it practically ruined him.

Still, murder went against the new leaf the President
had turned since the earthquake destroyed Haiti. The media and, even more important, Haitian word of mouth
for the most part praised his sangfroid, compassion, and,
to everyone's surprise, eloquence in helping the people
deal with the tragedy and traumas that followed. In mar-
shaling resources around the world to help the country
figure out how to pick up the pieces, the President had
been darn-right heroic. Haiti had developed faith in its
president after years of familiarity, a first in the country's
history.

In the lobby of the United Nations, the President's cabinet greeted him with desperate, searching eyes. Although
the President had gotten sick and thrown up during the
elevator ride down after the meeting with Satan and his
kitchen cabinet, the humiliating ritual did generate good
news for the fate of Haiti. The superfriends would pro-
vide resources for Haiti's resource-free government and
send armies armed with potential relief for the victims
of nature's freakiness. The President gave the guys the
thumbs-up. They jumped for joy. He had secured billions

of dollars in grants and low-interest loans from the American and his friends, to be funneled through United Nations agencies and other nongovernmental organizations to rebuild Haiti. Build back better, they said. The President watched his cabinet high-five and hug each other. The President was careful to avoid hugging anyone. He didn't want them to smell the vomit on his breath.

In the euphoria, the President also decided he didn't want Destiné dead for sleeping with his wife. Part of him did. Really, really did. But when the President considered the order he'd given Bobo, regret gave his heart an acidity he longed to erase. He couldn't help but try to distance himself from it. He didn't want Destiné dead, he decided, just roughed up. A warning. So he would finally stay away from Natasha for good. If that hardheaded boy would not obey such a reasonable message, the President would come up with an alternative solution that would be effective but not deadly.

Murdering Alain Destiné would have been the first time I've used my power as head of state to try to give myself a small amount of pleasure. Would God forgive me for this sin? Will God forgive me anything? I am doing the right thing for millions of others. Belatedly, but still. Will my immortal soul pay for this one indulgence if I manage, in my final act as a public servant, to corral commitments to bring food and water and medicine in a timely fashion to millions of people who are hungry, unemployed, without homes, and living in the bull's-eye of a host of coming rainy seasons, deadly diseases, and natural disasters?

When the President was finally alone in his suite at the Warwick Hotel a few hours later, he groped for an answer to the right moral choice despite his aggrieved pride. He got on his knees by his bedside, a habit of well-bred boys he'd acquired, and he said the Lord's Prayer. He took a hot shower, put on pajamas, and crawled into bed. The team had made him promise to check out the news to see sound bites from the press conference he'd participated in at the UN that afternoon, so he turned on the eleven o'clock news. He watched the American president announce the humanitarian financial package the international community had pledged to help Haiti, our neighbor and friend in its darkest hour, come out from under the rubble and chaos caused by the earthquake "better than ever before." The Haitian president flashed back to a chart some United Nations Development Programme consultant had showed him estimating the earthquake had generated as much rubble as twenty World Trade Centers. It took New York City one entire year to clear the rubble of its ground zero, and nearly ten years later they had yet to finish constructing a worthy replacement, and that disaster was located in the center of one of the wealthiest cities in the world with access to the best and biggest trucks, the widest streets, and state-of-the-art dump sites, construction experts, architects, engineers, and technologists. If politics and grief could paralyze mighty New York, how much time will Haitians need to clear the chunks of concrete littering their towns when all they have are bare hands, mighty hearts, and traffic-clogged streets and zero public awareness of the concept of a dump site and pooling resources for collective sustainable development? How would the people of Léogâne, Carrefour, and Port-au-Prince muster the patience and strength to spend the next twenty years sanding down, cleaning up, and rebuilding streets when food, health care, education, and care for their children will also be concerns without regular relief? The President had no answer, and no answer came to him while he knelt and bowed his head in his hotel room. How diminutive and frail and hot under the collar that consultant back then, like the American president today, made him feel by his disparity of know-how and resources in the face of such a great challenge. The President rushed to the bathroom to vomit. While worshipping the porcelain god, he had an epiphany about the frailties of the Haitian condition and the coping devices his people, particularly, their men, had relied on over centuries and generations to gain and maintain a little dignity. The President hunted down a Haitian radio station on the AM dial and found a syrupy Roger Colas song he hadn't heard in years, "Tu peux compter sur moi." *Sur qui?* the President wondered. *Sur Lui? Ou lui? Lui et moi?* And for the first time in his long, tough life, the President felt a tinge of pity for someone other than himself. Out of the seeds of pity grew a wave of warm kindness and affection for a collective that had come to be symbolized by the face and fate of one stupid young man. He picked up his Black-Berry and he wrote Bobo.

It is extremely important that Alain Destiné is not harmed under any circumstance. Arrange to have him medivaced to Miami for treatment of his injuries as soon as possible. I'll be home tomorrow.

Alain Destiné would live, the President decided, or at least not die by his hand. He'll lose permanently his right to live in Haiti, but he'll get to keep his life. The boy, like most of us, had lost enough things that mattered in his young life. Not least of which will be the woman he loved, my wife.

PART IV

God is our refuge and strength, a very present
    help in trouble.
Therefore will not we fear, though the earth
    be removed, and though the mountains be
    carried into the midst of the sea;
though the waters thereof roar and be
    troubled, though the mountains shake with
    the swelling thereof. Selah.
There is a river, the streams whereof shall
    make glad the city of God, the holy place of
    the tabernacles of the most High.
God is in the midst of her; she shall not be
    moved: God shall help her, and that right
    early.
The heathen raged, the kingdoms were
    moved: he uttered his voice, the earth
    melted.
        —Psalm 46

The glory of He who moves everything penetrates the universe and shines in one part more and, in another, less. This idea, learned from Dante, of course, had energized Natasha in the past and fueled her faith. It made her feel like she visited heaven when creating art, a heaven that took most of His light. And now she had seen things that should not be told, and she thought, What I was able to store up of that holy kingdom in my imagination may not be enough to get through my travails and life.

More or less around the time her husband, a veteran cynic, and her boyfriend, a robust atheist, experienced fresh sparks of faith, the object of their affections, a self-proclaimed Caribbean-born daughter of Dante and the most devout Catholic they knew, lost her faith in the fog of disaster. The fog of natural disasters had a lot in common with the more well known fog of war. The confusion caused by the chaos of war and battle, which had been practically patented by the Americans since World War II, shrouded Port-au-Prince. The notable difference between the fog of disaster and the fog of war, however, may be that the state of perplexity created by natural disasters comes with the added deprivation of a specific asshole for victims and revenge-seekers to blame for their rotten luck. The pacifying anger that comes from blaming other nationalities, ethnic groups, or religions for stunning sudden losses escapes those struck by disaster. So does its temporary relief from grieving and rebuilding. Without righteous rage, what are you left with? Are you reduced to a baby's pre-sentient state of frustration? In this new near-fetal position, Natasha struggled to keep a handle on her sanity. Guilt, furthermore, braided through her memories of the very flawed adult she had become. She had reason to believe her boyfriend had died because she locked him in the closet in a room near the top of a building the earthquake had brought low. As if practically killing the man she loved wasn't enough, her cuckolded husband's subsequent surge of courage and strength in the face of the calamity that befell their island further shamed her. Regret and sadness made her feel like a living scarlet letter. Alain died because of me. My husband was a good man I treated shabbily. There's nothing I can do to change any of those things. Heaven will have no place for me. Why am I still alive and not in the appropriate circle of hell for adulteresses? Why? The answer had yet to arrive despite her vigils under a weeping statue of Jesus on a cross in the cathedral she had chosen to call home since the disaster. After the earthquake, survivors had moved to live everywhere and anywhere around town and the countryside. They lived in parks, mostly, but also in yards and gardens and golf courses and soccer fields. Natasha made her home in the dark and dank catacombs of the National Cathedral. The cathedral's tone of grave and perpetual mourning matched her mood well. Like a giant tomb. Strangely, no other survivors joined her. Her only company was a dying old priest who slept in a cot in his former office in the decapitated church.

They sat together in the lone room with a roof, bathed, during the day, by light filtered to a rainbow kaleidoscope of hues by a stained-glass window. When not crying or praying, Natasha passed the time listening to Monsignor Dorélien, wondering how she screwed up her shot at heaven so completely when life's fragility should have given her better ways to spend the finite time she had. How could you have forgotten to be grateful for the loves in your life? How could you abuse them so? Monsignor Dorélien, for his part, simply wished the child would eat something.

You should go out and find him, the priest said out of the blue one afternoon.

You should rest, Natasha said.

What's today's date? He asked.

February fourteenth, she said.

Ah, it's Valentine's Day, he said. Is that why you're so grumpy? You miss him, don't you?

Who?

The boy.

You mean, my husband.

No, I mean the man you love more than Jesus.

Father, you blaspheme. That's not funny.

Monsignor Dorélien started to laugh, but the mirth got blocked by his collapsed lungs and reverted to a cough, a choked rattle so violent it scared away the black vultures that had been waiting on top of the church's pink walls for his corpse.

You should leave me be, the priest whispered once his coughing fit subsided, exhausted. I'm done. I'll die as soon as your sad eyes turn away.

I can't, the young girl whispered, eyes welling with affection.

The priest, who was gray like a damp sheet and so close to death you could almost see the angels standing guard check their watches, lifted a trembling hand and placed it on Natasha's hand. The girl grasped the hand so hard it almost hurt him. This is new, the priest thought. Since Natasha Robert had been a child she had one quirk: she hated to be touched. She was a wonderfully pleasant girl. She was quick, kind, and pretty, with flowing heaps of curly hair that attracted people's attention like bees to honey. She also had the pretty girl's desire to deflect attention, to be seen as a madonna and not a doll or trophy. Of all the orphans and young people Monsignor Dorélien had taken under his wing in his sixty-year career, Natasha

Robert was unique in that she asked for precious little—from the church, God, or her fellow man, especially men. Instead, she was a giver, an eager-to-pleaser. She gave kindness, inspiration, sympathy, and humor. She strove to give her community beauty. She yearned for security and the comfort of reliable routine, like everyone else, but she did not actively seek it from the people around her. We are all children and would prefer to behave like children at our happiest, the priest knew, but this child, by fate or nurture, worked hard to hide her inner child, even when she had been a child and had every right to petulance and selfishness. Once she entered the cathedral that fateful day as a preteen, she developed into something of an actress. She liked to pretend to play the role of the charitable adult in charge that most of us often avoided or performed clumsily. She was a sweetheart at it as long as you didn't touch her.

Something had changed in the child since the disaster, Monsignor Dorélien feared. When she found him buried alive in his office in the back of the cathedral, she had summoned all her strength, and God's grace with more than a few deargodhelpmes, to pull cement blocks off him as quickly as she could. Which was natural and typical of Natasha, Monsignor Dorélien knew. What was new was the desperation and pitch of her cries for help once her strength began to falter. Those cries were heartrending. Monsignor Dorélien almost wished he had died so he could have been spared hearing the anguish in the child's voice that day. The men who eventually joined her in saving what little of him was left under the unbearable embrace of the massive slabs of granite seemingly doubled their efforts to quiet the hysterical child.

For a long while afterward, the girl stared at the wounded priest in dumbfounded silence. She seemed elated that her prayers for his rescue had come true, but she couldn't understand why her prayers for others', notably Alain's, did not. The ideas of atheists sneaked up on her. Life was just a game. Life had no deeper meaning for humans than it had for animals. There was no heaven, and there certainly was no hell. There was no God. There was good luck and there was bad luck. Luck was to be prepared for and seized or frittered away. Bad luck was meant to be endured and shrugged off. Everything passed with time. There are an awful lot of coincidences. Blame yourself for your poverty. Credit your genes, genius, and moxie for your wealth. Hate Dad. Beauty was mathematical. Making money was art. What money bought best were toys. Evolve or get out of the way. What about the conscience? she thought. What did the atheists have to say about the source of pangs of guilt, and the soul, that stupid, bigger-than-you essence of yourself that craved harmony and love with everything and everyone in its environment? Where do they seek comfort in the days after everything they believed in, like justice and love, has fallen apart or disappeared altogether? Things don't fall apart just in Africa. They fall apart everywhere. Everywhere. Anytime.

I wasn't ready for the apocalypse, she said.

What apocalypse? Monsignor Dorélien said.

You know, the earthquake, Father, the slight twitch of dirt that killed almost everyone we loved in the city the other day.

Child, please. That wasn't the apocalypse. Do you believe that after the apocalypse, you'd still have the luxury to sit around and feel sorry for yourself? Here I thought you'd finally lost the rose-colored glasses you wore all the time.

But, Father, if that disaster wasn't the apocalypse, an end of all things, what was it? Punishment? That's what some people believe, you know.

A test, child. Goudou-goudou was a test. That's all it was. A test. You've read your share of Bible stories. You know God puts the people he loves the most through the worst sacrifices. If you ask me, this is one of the easiest tests we've faced in a long time.

The priest chuckled, then coughed.

Why do you say that, Father?

Well, for one, it wasn't subtle. It was so loud I still can't hear anyone more than a meter away from me. Every Haitian alive knows it happened, got its message, and responded to it in a way that revealed the limits and strengths of their character and faith. They now know full well how to improve their standing with God and Jesus based on their behavior. Jesus still loves them, but they will find lying about who they are and could be to themselves much harder. Second, the damage the earthquake caused was mostly physical! Rebounding from physical loss, even on that scale, should be a piece of cake for a people who so ably recovered from decades of slavery. The old Port-au-Prince was a city they inherited. The new city will be the one they create for themselves. It's a rare opportunity to start over fresh. You don't get many of those in this life. Can they? Can you? It's not a bad question. You could be facing worse challenges, you know.

Intellectually, that makes sense. Emotionally the whole thing is baffling.

I know it is. Which leads to my third point: the earthquake was the latest sign that God loves Haiti.

He what?

He loves you. Of course God loves Haitians. Why else would He encourage us to keep our faces pressed against the windows of great American and European wealth and grandeur, so close yet so cruelly far, like a nation of Holly Golightlys? Why else would He chin-check us every couple of years with trying natural disasters—an earthquake here, a few hurricanes there, with a dash of floods? Why else would He constantly tempt our rich and powerful to be corrupted by short-term profits in an almost barren world? Finally, why else, dear child, would God make our life so hard yet so sweet on an island so beautiful yet so, so fragile? Think about it: The moral of most stories in the Bible is that God's chosen people, Adam, Eve, Abraham, the whole lot, will constantly be asked by Him to make the greatest personal sacrifices possible to honor His mysterious glory. The way we Haitians suffer misfortune, deprivation, and disproportionate foreign enmity is right in line with the fate of chosen peoples throughout history. Biblically speaking anyway. God may love us too much, I'd say.

The old priest was either completely daft, Natasha thought, or taking her to a deeper understanding of things than she could handle at her age and in her current frazzled state. Before Monsignor Dorélien could continue his sermon for one, a boom filled the room. A strong breeze from an opened-and-slammed door rushed in. Candles flickered. Dorélien gave Natasha the nod to go see who had entered the church. Natasha walked into the large main hall and stood next to the altar. For the first time in a long time, she felt no fear. One reason she'd sought refuge inside a severely damaged church despite public warnings for all Haitians to avoid going inside buildings before they were inspected by the authorities on account of the risk of aftershocks was because she secretly dug the idea of being killed by a cathedral's tumbling walls. There was something artful about getting buried alive by a cathedral. Maybe even having her head crushed or heart speared by a toppled crucifix.

In the church that evening, however, Natasha was in no mood to die. She felt fine, with the first glimmers of inspiration for her life's next act. A test? she thought. She liked tests. Miraculously, the tears that seemed permanently painted in the corner of her eyes had dissipated. She turned her back to the altar and faced . . . a mob. About twenty young men holding candles and megaphones and shovels in their hands stood at the end of the cathedral's long hall. They looked to be in various stages of exhaustion. They were laborers, gravediggers, probably, and their day had been long. Once they saw her, they erupted in song. They sang a hymn of beauty and optimism with such vigor Natasha clutched her chest:

> *O Lord my God! When I in awesome wonder*
> *Consider all the worlds Thy hands have made.*
> *I see the stars, I hear the rolling thunder,*
> *Thy power throughout the universe displayed.*

> *Then sings my soul, my Savior God, to Thee;*
> *How great Thou art, how great Thou art!*
> *Then sings my soul, my Savior God, to Thee:*
> *How great Thou art, how great Thou art!*

> *When through the woods and forest glades I wander*
> *And hear the birds sing sweetly in the trees;*
> *When I look down from lofty mountain grandeur*
> *And hear the brook and feel the gentle breeze:*

> *And when I think that God, His Son not sparing,*
> *Sent Him to die, I scarce can take it in;*
> *That on the cross, my burden gladly bearing,*
> *He bled and died to take away my sin:*

When Christ shall come with shouts of acclamation
And take me home, what joy shall fill my heart!
Then I shall bow in humble adoration,
And there proclaim, my God, how great Thou art!

The young men sang like angels. Their clothes stank to high heavens. Yes, they were gravediggers. The foul smell that came from their sweat as they sang confirmed it. Natasha had heard rumors about a group of men from the outskirts of Pétionville near a soccer field in a valley. After the earthquake, these men had organized themselves into a brigade that took charge of policing and protecting survivors living in camps and finding help. Incredibly, they earned people's trust by burying, free of charge, the stacks of dead, often decomposing, corpses that littered the neighborhoods. We have to do it for ourselves was their motto. Their leader this night stepped toward Natasha, but not too far forward, for he knew he carried the stench of hundreds of dead bodies. Jean-Richard Souvenir, he said. Natasha hesitated to say her name. They might recognize it, and she'd jeopardize one of the myriad security protocols of the first lady of Haiti. Bah, they probably don't read the papers much, she thought.

Natasha Robert, she said.

We're sorry for disturbing you, madame.

That was some entrance.

We sing when we enter a room at night to let people around know we mean no harm.

Outside, the day had slipped into night without Natasha's noticing. A full moon hung overhead, silver and cheesy. Natasha felt hungry and horny for the first time in a long time; the appetites of the normal had taken over her body where depression had ruled. Fleetingly, Natasha wondered what making love to twenty strapping young gravediggers in the church's pews would feel like.

That hymn was written from a nineteenth-century Swedish poem, Souvenir said.

So they do know how to read, Natasha thought. Shit. They know who I am.

Come in, she said. Sit, sit. Make yourselves comfortable. You look tired. You must be exhausted. I'll get you some water. I have no food, just some bread.

That's OK, Souvenir said. We picked up some *fritailles* before we came. We don't want to trouble you. We only wish to bunk for the night.

There are *marchands de fritailles* working already?

Yes, ma'am.

This was the first good news from the city outside the cathedral Natasha had gotten in days, too many days for her to remember. Small fried food stands were running! That's terrific news. Was it possible that birds would soon start singing again, lovers start caressing and arguing, and live bands start inspiring slow-dancing to return as the national pastime? Over fried pork chunks, plantains, and sugared water, the men ate in silence and shared what they could with Natasha. When the first bellies felt satisfied, their owners began to banter. They joked about some of the most elaborate funerals they remembered. They talked of tombs that were bigger and more stylishly designed than many houses. How common it was to see a woman who lived in a shack be buried in a minicastle.

When Natasha chimed in, mouth full and fingers greasy, she wondered why, with all the funerals that were surely taking place around town these days, no one came to the cathedral for services. A silence fell with the thud of an iron gate. One man got up and walked away, disappearing into one of the pitch-black corners of the church. Another did the same. Many lowered their heads or looked away. Most looked to Souvenir to speak. The moment was awkward. You could hear rats skitter for crumbs across the marble floor.

First we tried to identify the dead, Souvenir said. His voice echoed around the church. We really tried, but there were too many. The smell was making everyone sick. It wasn't just us. The government, business owners, everyone who owned a truck, it seemed, helped, pitched in, but there were too many corpses. Too, too many. The best we could do was keep a running tally on sheets of paper as we scooped corpses with loaders and deposited them in dump trucks.

Dump trucks?

Yes, dump trucks.

One of the men flung a beer bottle against a wall in disgust. *Mon Dieu*, forgive us, another said. Another crossed himself.

To be fair, some families did come retrieve bodies along the way, Souvenir continued. Those that could afford to bought pretty caskets and draped them with flowers. They drove their dead themselves to a crematory or family plots, God bless them.

Amen, said an older man sitting in the pew next to Jean-Richard Souvenir.

Those who had no money burned the bodies themselves, Souvenir said. Initially we tried to wrap all the dead tightly in pink and white sheets stripped from beds or salvaged from the rubble, and then carefully placing them on sidewalks for loading. Soon, even relatives who had spent days digging up their dead were too tired to care about what happened to them. They placed them on the sidewalks. We picked them up and went looking for places, and then we buried the bodies. We did what we could. It wasn't pretty.

And some people criticized us for it, said the man who had walked away upon return. His face lit up close by yellow candlelight. Us!

The prime minister said the country cleared some hundred thousand bodies in the first five days alone. Can you imagine a hundred thousand dead bodies in one city like that? And we barely scratched the surface. Léogâne's dead have barely been touched. There are more bodies all over the streets.

So many more, someone else said.

Who knows how many.

The government really did try to figure out how to best handle all the dead bodies after goudou-goudou. We all wanted to find an alternative to putting bodies on loaders and having loaders put bodies in trucks, and having trucks take bodies to improvised dump sites, like so much trash. Those people deserved better. But the bodies were beginning to decompose, to smell. We were facing a choice: leave them in the streets to rot where you would never be able to identify them and run the risk of making people living around them sick, or leave with them and bury them wherever we could, as well as we could. We all decided to put the safety of those people who are still alive ahead of better treatment of the dead.

Who gave you the right, huh? the Angry Man said, angrily. Who?

The Fort National cemetery was quickly filled beyond capacity, Souvenir said after a sympathetic glance at Angry Man. There were bodies on top of bodies on top of tombs.

All the men shook their heads at the memory. One looked like he wanted to literally shake the memory out of his head. Natasha listened with her mouth open.

The earthquake demolished a lot of tombs, so what we did was, we broke into tombs to create mass graves. It was the simplest solution for us to quickly remove the bodies from the streets.

Angry Man sucked his teeth loudly.

Some people are upset, Souvenir said. The government

buried five thousand bodies in a landfill in Titanyen, then the people living in the neighborhood near it started protesting. The government had to quickly find another location while trucks loaded with bodies stood still. The government designated a new site. People started dumping bodies there, on the road near there, on the road to go there, everywhere, without even burying them. We've been burying those bodies to protect the locals from diseases. We all wish things worked out differently. Jesus Christ, why couldn't we have more body bags at least?

Angry Man walked away again and disappeared into the darkness on the other side of the cathedral. His sobs wafted through the pews seconds later. The sobs were heavy and watery.

See that man? Souvenir said to Natasha, pointing into the blackness where sobs flowed like beat-boxing. That man buried fourteen family members with his own hands over two days after goudou-goudou. Wife, children, nieces, uncles, and his parents.

Natasha, an orphan, stared at the darkness and tried to imagine what having fourteen relatives to love and live near could be like, and how horrible having to bury them all at once could feel. She almost fainted.

The next morning, the brilliant heat of the sun stunned Natasha awake despite the fact that she slept under a pew with her forearm shielding her face. You think you miss not having a roof over your head when it rains? When you're trying to sleep in after a long night of dreaming of hurriedly discarded dead bodies, not having a roof sucks almost as bad. Around Natasha, the guys were awake too. But they looked like they'd had the good night's sleep Natasha wished she'd had. Their energy was high, in midday form. Clean-shaven, showered, and pumped from performing push-ups and crunches, not smiling but faintly upbeat, they were gentlemen who tried not to look at the train wreck Natasha no doubt looked like. In the bathroom—yes, the bathroom had no roof, yet, oddly, the toilet still flushed—Natasha took stock in the mirror. She did indeed look like shit. Her hair went everywhere and nowhere and begged for the mercy of a drop of shampoo. The rest of her could use a proper, long, and languid wash too instead of the splashes of cold water and the touch of a microcube of soap. This is not how you want to look when you're going to see the man who could have been your father-in-law on the day of the memorial of his son's death, Natasha thought. At least her clothes were relatively clean, her breasts firm and high, and her face unblemished, chocolate skin looking brand-new. She checked in on Monsignor Dorélien. He was enjoying having the gravediggers around.

In many ways we are in the same business, he said.

A few of them listened to him intently as he talked about the importance of honoring the dead and how they shouldn't make much of the absence of the rituals of service he specialized in for the dead. My work was elaborate and a welcome succor in normal times. In these times, these men will have to count on the purity of the love in their hearts and the talent they pour into their work to stand as the symbol of the rite of passage for those thousands of folks who have gone on to meet their maker without the comfort of a coffin and a tombstone. Before they left, they all closed their eyes, and Monsignor Dorélien blessed them and their families for their courage and faith. Natasha watched the men stream out of Monsignor Dorélien's small office with chins high. Today was the national day of mourning for the victims of goudou-goudou. The government had declared a weekend period of memorial. Millions were expected to converge on the National Palace and the Champ de Mars to sing and pray and cry for their collective and individual losses. A nation of stoics was about to have a very public mass catharsis. The gravediggers were eager for it. Most people were. Natasha was too. They, the living, wanted to touch and to be touched. Mourning was such a lonely business. Today, sorrow would be shared. Natasha planned to pay her respects to the dead by visiting an elderly couple she knew to be too old to make the trip from their hilltop home to the Champ de Mars.

Are you sure about this? Jean-Richard asked for the fifth time.

They were standing on the steps of the National Cathedral. His confreres stood a few meters away. They were all clean and eager to join the ceremonies, which, Haiti being Haiti, would have a carnivalesque flair. Natasha

would be going in the opposite direction, in a car provided by her new friends. You're not even going to wait
for your security guards to come take you? Jean-Richard
asked. Is that wise?

This is not an affair of state, Natasha said. Everyone
has the right to mourn their dead this day their own way.
Besides, with everyone downtown today, going the opposite direction will be the safest direction to go in the
entire city.

All right, Madame Robert, he said.

Natasha, she said.

Madame Natasha, he said with a smile.

They hugged farewell. The man was all muscle, Natasha thought, her chin on his shoulder. Thanks for everything, she said. Squinting into the morning sun, she
waved good-bye to the rest of the fellas. *Au revoir*, they
said, *et merci*! She watched them join the crowd one by
one, brown heads and arms bobbing, red, yellow, black,
green shirts and dresses, hats and caps and fans a-waving.
The gravediggers could be anyone now, lost among the
living. They couldn't be happier. She was happy for them.

The car was old and looked unsafe. It may have been
yellow once. Today the car was a sickly beige-and-white
with echoes of a mustard past. There were no windows
but there were a windshield and leather seats. Very hot
leather seats. Took a while for the car to start, a dozen tries
of the ignition, enough to make Natasha's wrist sore. The
engine wheezed and seemed to ask why Natasha wanted it

to make the effort of waking up. Like a metallic wounded horse, the car seemed to want to sit there, ready to be put to sleep or somehow be nursed to health.

Come on, car, Natasha said. I don't have all day.

The crowds walking by the car toward the Champ de Mars grew thin. Songs and prayers began to waft along the morning breeze from down the street. The festivities were off and running. The dead were no doubt smiling. Some of them in heaven were probably pointing fingers at Natasha and having a laugh. Some people looked into the car and at Natasha and then asked her if she needed help, a push, something. No, no, she said, waving them off.

After a while people looked at her like she was crazy to believe the car would start at any point that day or crazy to want to drive the vomit-colored pile of junk in the first place. Miracle of miracles, the car started. Easing into the street, Natasha saw fewer and fewer people. Fort National had been severely hit by the earthquake. Buildings looked like bombed-out skeletons. Natasha could see dead bodies inside them. Corpses propped up to sitting position. By who? For what? In front of some other buildings, she saw corpses in the usual positions, flat on their backs and wrapped up, mummified. She sped up. In front of the Musée du Panthéon National Haïtien, off the Champ de Mars, she saw mothers and grandmothers and fathers and sons and daughters embrace. Everyone, it seemed, had an arm wrapped over another's shoulders, eyes shut tight in prayer. After a while, she turned onto Avenue Ducoste.

Where the Air France store once stood as a symbol of the great world off the island, Natasha saw only two stories of gray rubble. She also saw a woman on her knees praying to the sky with two plane tickets in her hands. Natasha crossed herself. There but for the grace of God go I, she said. She dared not imagine how those tickets, Air France, and the earthquake had hurt that woman. She dared not. Before long, Natasha had to make a left turn on Chemin des Dalles, and then a right turn on Avenue John Brown. Big like its namesake, Avenue John Brown was orderly this day. Some foot traffic headed toward the Champ de Mars. Most people sat pensively on wooden chairs at storefronts. Not for the first time, Natasha noticed the Haitian flags. They were everywhere and bigger and, for some reason, redder, whiter, and bluer than she ever remembered. Avenue John Brown was also called Lalue, and it was where Natasha and Bobo had seen the fearsome crowd and tried to rescue the small boy from getting trampled. What happened to you, young man? Natasha thought. Where are you now? I hope you're safe.

Lalue then went through Bourdon, an upmarket neighborhood. Stalls selling sculptures made of cans and hubcaps lined the sidewalk behind which was a deadly cliff. Natasha couldn't help naming the streets and took pleasure in the bumps and grinds of their potholes, as if for the first time. She was renewing her relationship with the street, the city, the earth, and so far, so good. You only get one hometown, she thought. You should be grateful to be alive in yours, Natasha. Turning left on rue Marcadieu, she soon reached Delmas 40B, and then she couldn't help egging the Datsun to go faster eastward, toward Pétion-ville. Around Delmas 95, she got stuck behind a giant United Nations peacekeepers' tank. The destroyed Carib-bean Market came up on her right. Since goudou-goudou, people couldn't stop talking about the destruction of this grand institution, although most Haitians couldn't afford to shop in it. Despite her efforts, Natasha couldn't help but imagine the serene scene inside the supermarket the minute before goudou-goudou. A supermarket late in the afternoon in any decent neighborhood in the world is a cool buzz of active mothers and fathers and children picking up vegetables, drinks, condiments, and cereal for the night's dinner and the next day's breakfast. It's adults forgetting the stresses of the day in favor of prosaic issues like sex and good meals and homework and trifling TV sitcoms. It's children enjoying a break between the tyr-anny of school and homework to release pent-up energy in slick aisles while begging for candy and cookies and looking forward to riding a sugar high home. All those people were completely crushed by the supermarket and buried inside it because of the earthquake. When people talked about the many iconic buildings ground to dust by the earthquake—the Palais de Justice, the midwives' school, the National Palace—they rarely failed to note that the supermarket had to have been at full capacity when goudou-goudou came.

At the corner of Delmas where Pétionville started, Natasha saw the old cemetery, the one that was destroyed, not by Mother Nature, but by mother mayor, a public servant with oversized renovation plans. Rue Metellus was empty. Some storefronts had their usual crowds. Where would men hang out in the middle of the day if they couldn't hang out at garages? But most shops and restaurants were closed for the day, a strange sight, for this was usually a very busy intersection. I guess people really needed that day off, Natasha thought. God bless them.

At Place Boyer, she had to slow down and start looking for a parking spot. Poking her head inside Brasserie Quartier Latin, the fancy restaurant favored by foreigners, Natasha saw a group of them drinking and laughing at a table on a veranda. Why should they be mourning anything? Natasha thought. To hear Jean-Richard tell it, Haiti's disaster answered many of their prayers for wealth, international adventure, and temporary sanctity. They tended to work in Haiti mostly on three-month assignments, so most of them would be returning to their less sanctimonious selves soon enough. That's what happens to people when they go home. Nothing humbles like home.

The villa on Place Boyer where Alain Destiné was born and raised by his doting father, Villard, and his artist mother, Katherine, was not necessarily the grandest villa by Pétionville's standards, but it was stately, with towering hedges of hibiscus and looming centuries-old almond trees, a riot of fragrant reds, pinks, and greens. Its most famous feature, of course, was the bookstore on the corner, Librarie Sidney-Nina. Named after dear expatriated cousins of Katherine's, the store featured the smartest collection of books by Haitian authors in English, French, Spanish, and even Creole in the city, as Alain had once bragged to Natasha. Everyone from Jacques Roumain to Georges Anglade to Dany Laferrière not only had his entire bibliography stocked there, the authors also visited often, mainly to chat with Alain's dad. A voluble raconteur with more than a passing resemblance to Harry Belafonte, Villard Destiné knew everything about everything in Haiti's cultural history. If he liked a customer well enough, he might break out a bottle of five-star Rhum Barbancourt to share a drink or five and insist that customer take the books he was browsing home as a gift. On this day, Librarie Sidney-Nina was closed.

The green gate of the villa creaked after Natasha pushed it in. The driveway had a black Range Rover that, judging from its blanket of white dust and dry leaves, had not been driven or cleaned in a while. The windows on the second and third floors of the villa were filled with cobwebs. Natasha was nervous. Unsure what kind of welcome she'd get from Alain's parents, she walked carefully.

Allo? Allo? She said.

Go away!

Natasha saw Alain Destiné's father looking down on her from the first-floor balcony, and Villard was pointing a gun at her.

Get out of here! he said.

Mr. Destiné? she said. Mr. Destiné! What are you doing? Put the gun down.

What am I doing? I'm getting ready to shoot me a looter trespassing on my property. That's what I'm doing. The question is, what the fuck are you doing here? You're not welcome here.

I came, I came . . . to pay my respects, sir. I loved Alain too.

Alain's dad shot Natasha. And missed. Natasha screamed and ducked and ran around the driveway frantically, looking for cover. Natasha crouched behind the Range Rover on her knees and prayed to God and Jesus her savior to save her one more time, to tell her what to do with her life, how to make things right in her fucked-up life. Then the answer came. Villard shot two more times, missing widely.

Villard! *Qu'est-ce que tu fais?!*

It was Katherine, merciful, sweet, even-tempered Katherine, Alain's mom. Still hiding behind their car, Natasha heard Katherine try to calm her husband down. It's that bitch's fault we lost him, Villard said, crying. If it wasn't for her, he'd still be alive.

That's no reason to go lose your head like that, Papa, Katherine said softly. No reason at all.

That bitch . . .

I know . . .

That bitch . . . I told you she was trouble. I told you . . .

221

I know, Papa, I know, but Alain was in love with her. What could we do? You remember how you were at that age, when you were in love. You wanted to die for it too.

Your father almost killed me for it.

My mother wanted to poison your food.

Katherine, I'm sorry . . .

The couple embraced. They stood on the balcony holding each other for a long time in hushed silence. No parent should ever have to bury a child or have a child disappear without a trace during a sudden disaster. In the volcanic fire of his grief for his only son, Villard Destiné remembered how he'd told Alain over and over, all his life, that no matter what bad things happened to him, he was one of the lucky ones. They were a very fortunate family in a society where fortune favored precious few families. You must take the bad with the same equanimity that you take the good things that happen to you, son. No matter when you die, he often told his son, you'll have lived a happier and more fully loved life than most people your age in Haiti or most anywhere else in the world. Such a sentiment was much easier to say than to live, Villard had realized since the earthquake, for grief had taken hold of his overachieved and exhausted soul, and he found his rage against the machine of fate hard to shake.

Villard stopped aiming his gun at his son's girlfriend and squeezed his wife closer into his body. Villard and Katherine watched Natasha walk to her car, slowly, almost as if she welcomed a bullet in the back of her head.

She looked up briefly. In the unforgiving noon sun, they saw her young face. It was an unrecognizable mask of misery and tears. They waved good-bye to her, as if to say, You're forgiven.

Natasha nodded at them with a broken heart darted by gratitude and slid into her car. With shaking hands, she fumbled for a piece of paper in her bag. The address on it calmed her heart and reduced the tears streaming down her face from a shower to a sprinkle. She was going to go to the place she believed she should have gone years ago. She was going home. The address on the piece of paper was scribbled in Monsignor Dorélien's hard-to-read chicken scratch. It read: The Convent of Cinq Coins, Kenscoff.

HOMECOMING

The mother superior opened the door of the Convent of Cinq Coins and sighed. Natasha looked a wreck, like someone who had been crying nonstop for a couple of hours, but the mother superior had known her for as long as Natasha had known Monsignor Dorélien, and she took her in with a sea of wordless warmth. She had a nun, Sister Hopstaken, show Natasha to her room and told Natasha to make herself at home. The room was down a long blue hall and up a few wooden stairs. Natasha came to the convent expecting to live in a cell worthy of one of America's nightmarish prisons. Instead, she got a room with a small wooden desk topped with a black leather King James Bible and a bed with simple linens. Her new nun's robe hung on a hanger in a closet, and she began to change clothes. Outside her window, the view of Port-au-Prince was spectacular. On the best days, like today, Kenscoff was almost an hour's drive on top of Pétionville.

The quartier was the last posh neighborhood in Port-au-Prince, famous for its five-star restaurants and cold nights. It had been known to snow there. Kenscoff sat on a mountaintop overlooking lush rolling hills and plains. Looking through the window from her room, Natasha could see only a sea of white clouds this day, with glimpses of mountains and a smattering of houses that looked like tiny thatched huts. The Convent of Cinq Coins seemed to be located at the highest point of Kenscoff. The view was breathtaking and gave Natasha the feeling that she was floating above the earth, as if she had ascended to heaven without going through the messy convention of death. The only thing she heard in the house and outside was silence. Intense, monastic silence. For a girl from downtown Port-au-Prince, which was loud and rowdy even on Sunday mornings, the concept of silence—sustained, musical, opaque—was a rumor, a myth, too beautiful to ever believe it could exist in the city.

Of course, a knock at the room's door soon interrupted Natasha's reverie. The knock was soft. That was a distinction rarely lost to Natasha and completely appreciated.

Are you ready? the voice behind the door said.

Yes, I am, Natasha said.

Before she opened the door, Natasha tried to smooth out her look. There were no mirrors. She was a novice nun, and during her period of novitiate, she shouldn't have been allowed to wear the full nun's habit, but the convent seemed to have put her on a fast track, partly out of familiarity with Natasha's relationship with the Call, but mostly out of convenience. These were painful times for the community the Catholic Church in Haiti had dedicated itself to. A war for the country's soul could erupt if the church's work did not hold its own alongside the work being done by all the other stakeholders, old and new, that abounded in the country. Also, the convent had no alternative, intermediate clothing available for Natasha, so she wore the outfit of a full-fledged sister, and she couldn't help hoping she looked good in it. The black robe had to make her look skinnier at the very least. The white scarf made her look younger, like a child. Innocent. Mortal. A child in the service of the Lord.

Natasha followed Sister Hopstaken down another corridor to Mother Superior's office. The office was spare and severe, though Natasha liked seeing that Mother Superior was at least a Mac and not a PC person. Mother Superior may have been beautiful once. She was old, maybe in her early sixties, even seventies, the daughter of Italian parents from Cap Haitien who had been in Haiti so long the sun had tanned her to look like any thin Haitian with vaguely Latin roots.

There's a lot of work to do, she said, so let's run through all the requirements for you to become a Catholic sister, OK, Sister Robert?

Yes, ma'am.

The marriage?

Will be annulled as soon as the justice department offices reopen. My husband will respect my decision, I'm sure of it.

Children?

None.

Pregnant?

No.

Good. The boyfriend?

Dead, Natasha said calmly.

Mother Superior showed no emotions.

Debts?

None whatsoever. In fact, I have a few unsold paintings left that could bring money to the church if . . .

Thank you, Sister Robert. That's for another day.

Mother Superior turned to Sister Hopstaken. This novitiate will be assigned to you for preparation for her first vows, Sister. In case you and the other sisters wonder why Sister Robert was so readily accepted by our convent, let me you tell you why. I've known her since she was a wayward child who appeared on Monsignor Dorélien's doorstep out of nowhere. She heard the Call, but God had also given her a gift, the gift of artistry, the muse. The muse put her in conflict with the Call. The muse seduced. The Call demanded. As is common with most young people, the muse won over Sister Robert for many years. It brought her a certain amount of fame and wealth and the attention of many, many suitors. She was lost to the church. I prayed for her. Monsignor Dorélien prayed for her. And now she's finally ready to listen to the Call and serve God.

Natasha thought she couldn't have summed up her life better. Dear Lord, she thought, Monsignor Dorélien must have been briefing Mother Superior about me all the time. He probably called her soon as I left the cathedral this morning.

The phone rang. After a minute of listening, Mother Superior said, Yes, Father, then she hung up. She turned to Sister Robert and Sister Hopstaken and almost smiled. Almost. Sister Robert, she said, your first test has already arrived. You are to return to the cathedral and help Monsignor Dorélien perform a wedding ceremony.

Yes, Mother Superior, Natasha said, feeling more certain than ever about the rightness of her choice and her capacity to fulfill the covenant's demands for the rest of her life. No doubt. Not a shred.

A few hours later, in the long shadows of a late afternoon in the steaming Caribbean winter, a beat-up Datsun parked on rue Dr. Aubry. Out came two nuns, one of whom, Sister Robert, walked awkwardly in her new robe. Her worst nightmare at that moment was that her flowing black robe would get stuck in a door or on a tree branch and accidentally be ripped off her body, leaving her nude in front of a shocked public. Paranoid doesn't necessarily mean careful, she realized, for as soon as she closed the car's door, the tail of her nun's habit became caught in it. Fortunately for her, she was

moving slowly enough to avoid disaster. Sister Hopstaken, meanwhile, was distracted by the full view of
the disaster their city had endured. The collapsed Notre
Dame de l'Assomption Catholic cathedral crouched in
front of her and beckoned shock, awe, and terror. Be
careful, Sister, Natasha said as Sister Hopstaken walked
toward the jagged piles in front of the cathedral as if in a
trance. Sister Hopstaken struggled to find a way around
the pile of rubble in the area of the back door entrance to
the cathedral. The older nun was about to fall and truly
hurt herself until the young one took her by the elbow
and said, I know another way in. It'll be easier.

They walked around the corner and climbed a smaller
pile and entered the church. Inside, there was a crowd.
They were dressed in what passed for their Sunday best
these days. Their clothes were free of that terrorizing
white dust. Is it safe to be here? Sister Hopstaken said,
looking nervously at the destroyed church from the inside
for the first time. It's the safest place in the world, Natasha
said.

The cathedral didn't have much of a roof left. What
was left of the once majestic hall was crumbled and split
apart. People sat on plastic chairs for the upcoming ceremony despite the obvious threat that whatever walls
were left standing could fall if the winds blew or the earth
caught another shiver. People sat on milk crates too, even
though the wall of the giant tower, the one filled with
giant snowflake-shaped windows of varying sizes, looked

shaky and worrisome. Turning away, Sister Robert looked her new colleague in the eyes and said with a resolve that came from a place deep inside and beyond her, God is good. The cathedral will not let us down this day. I'm sure of it. Let's go find Monsignor Dorélien.

WOMEN

Down in Place Pigeon, Alain Destiné was about to attend the same ceremony. He had undergone a resurrection of sorts. And he was excited. How do I look? he asked Hollywood. They were standing in the brown patch of dirt in front of Alain's tent, and the closest mirror available was buried in the palace across the street. You look like a man who just showered and shaved for the first time in a month, Hollywood said, grinning. You look like shit with makeup. And you could use a haircut.

You and your jokes, Alain said. Tasteful as usual. Xavier, *viens ici, mon petit*. How do I look?

Xavier smiled and gave Alain the thumbs-up. Alain wore the same clothes he'd worn during his crash-land in Place Pigeon. They were the only clothes he owned. He had had them washed by Yanick's girls, and, more notably, he had finally braved the communal showers in the middle of the refugee camp and washed himself up, even going so far as to shave off the beard that had combined with his bushy-dreadlocking afro to make him look a bit like Jesus. He shaved with a small shaving kit a matronly Swedish aid worker had suggestively slipped him a few days before. He had used deodorant, an environmentally-unfriendly spray, but it worked wonders, at least dampening the terrible smell he carried. Eradicating said smell would take many more showers, and to take that many showers as regularly as sanity demanded required Alain to take the long-overdue next steps of returning to his civilized life. Or at least to his parent's house, the next-best thing. Return home, to Papa and Maman, the house on Place Boyer. Engage Haiti's disaster recovery process from the rarefied airs inside the national and city governments and business communities that were his inheritance and not via the grass-free-roots level he had been working in since goudou-goudou. "Goudou-goudou." The onomatopoetic word Haitians used to describe the earthquake, or, more accurately, an approximation of the sounds the quaking earth had made as the ground made the things in their world rock back and forth and up and down. The word was primitive, but it had an accuracy and a musical quality Alain had come to enjoy. His appreciation of the small pleasures of life at the bottom of Port-au-Prince's society had grown in direct proportion to his dread to return to life among Haitian strivers without the company and the love of Natasha Robert to strive for. There had been no news of the first lady since goudou-

goudou. The news from the presidency centered around the work the President was doing or not doing enough of to secure food, medicine, and enterprise to help Haitians dig themselves out of the rubbled city God's belching earth had left behind. Fucking God, Alain thought. There was no God. There never was. There were tectonic plates deep beneath the sea. That's for sure. Shifty motherfuckers. There was human kindness, courage, and mortality. There were whole hosts of political and scientific reasons to explain Haiti and its dire circumstances. There was philosophy, to be sure. Every day Alain looked out at the reality surrounding his tent. The matrons braiding hair, the boys chasing balls, the girls looking proud yet nervous about their curves, the bored men, the resigned elders, the hurt, the sick, the troubled. The waiting for death. The fundamental nature of the reality we shared was no longer worth Alain's concern. His new religion was no religion. His new God was no God. Fuck God. There was death and there was life filled with micromoments to fill before death.

The idea of faith in an omnipresent, benevolent, and discrete deity may have dimmed in Alain in the wake of the earthquake, but the aggrieved romantic hung on to a soft spot for love, the very essence of Jesus, Christianity, Islam, Buddhism, any religion *digne du nom*. Which was the only available explanation for his excitement for the coming wedding, the first anyone had heard of in Haiti after the earthquake. These were not his nuptials. He had looked and smelled and sometimes behaved too much like a wounded sewer rat for far too long for a woman to look at him with anything other than concern, pity, or disgust. Besides, he told people he lost his wife during the earthquake, and he'd come to enjoy the persona of a widower. It wasn't a total lie. His one true love seemingly had died that day, vanished. Oh, how he'd give up a limb or two just to see Natasha again and scoop her up between his arms, but he was working hard to move on. Who chases a married woman, anyway? How foolish is that? He knew Natasha was gone, to her heaven on earth or beyond, and he was making himself be happy for her. If you love someone, set her free and all that. Philippe's getting married, and I'll live vicariously through him, Alain thought. His buddy Philippe, the refugee camp leader extraordinaire at Place Pigeon, deserved this happiness. He'd met a girl in some unfathomable corner of the Place Pigeon refugee camp one night and fallen in love. To Alain, it seemed fitting that Philippe's affection for their community would develop a sexual component. The camp's population had mushroomed from one thousand to twenty thousand seemingly overnight, and even though the ever-busy and dedicated socialist that was Philippe knew everyone and kept a running tally of who needed what help, he had somehow shoehorned in time to fall in love with a girl named Fabiola Georges. Fabiola was something else. The few times Alain had met her, at camp leadership council meetings—Fabiola

represented a group from the street on the other side of
the National Palace; they were wretched motherfuckers,
even in this collection of wretched of the earth—Fabby
immediately struck him as smarter than he and Philippe
and Hollywood put together. The first time they met, to
debate choosing among tarps for tents from different do-
nors, or whatever the fuck—Alain couldn't remember—
Fabby had made a point that was so spot-on, man, Alain
should've written it down. Hollywood poked Alain with
an elbow and whispered, Is that how y'all grow them
here? Jesus H. Christ, why couldn't I have found one of
those in Los Angeles?

Not that Hollywood had any problems getting women.
On an every-other-day basis, like clockwork, an international entertainment starlet or gorgeous philanthropist or
celebrity of some kind came around his tent for a visit. Part
sport, part PR move, Hollywood's Love Parade, as Alain
and Philippe had come to call it, was good for Place Pigeon's
business, though it didn't seem to do much for Hollywood's
spirits. If Alain was pitifully post-God from heartbreak,
Hollywood claimed to be post-love from the same.

I don't even jerk off anymore, Hollywood told Alain
one dawn after another of their all-night drinking binges/
vigils. What's the point? My imagination can't muster
anything transcendent anymore. Maybe I've lived too
long and fucked too many beautiful women.

Or maybe you've watched too much porn, Steve,
Alain said.

Yeah, that's it. Fucking porn, pun intended. Porn ruined me for women and sex. I can't even look at my right hand the same way anymore. I blame the Internet.

Yeah, Alain said, Steve Jobs should've stillborned the thing instead of making it so fucking fun to fuck with. iHate the fucking Internet too.

During the courtship, Philippe had come around Alain's tent almost every night to get their help deciphering the Chinese-puzzle-worthy, head-scratching signals of the Haitian woman. As though Alain, of all people, had a clue. Few women on this planet are more difficult to read than Haitian women, Alain's father had told him when he was too young to understand, though Papa's seriousness about the topic made Alain care. Trust me, son, Villard Destiné said, I've traveled the world and, er, broken bread with women from India, Africa, even *beurettes*, Europeans, Asians, Americans, and Latinas, women from all the way in the deepest jungles of the Amazon to the saunas in Iceland. No matter. You can't be loved like a Haitian woman loves, nor could you be dropped as completely and as coldly as when a Haitian woman's done with you. May you never experience such a cold, son. Cold like space. A vacuum that turns Caribbean homes into igloos.

Alain's father continued: Haitian women and their steel decisiveness mystified me like no other in much the same way they mystified my father, his father, and his father, and his father's father before him. We men, we debate. Women, they act. We sing. They make the drums.

We dither, lord, we dither. They build. My father did tell me that if I got more than second breath of *chaleur* from one, I should grab on to her mighty hips and never let go or bruise them. And my father was right, Alain. My subsequent brief brushes with these women's glorious sound and terrible fury convinced me. So I married the first fantastic Haitian woman who would have me and never looked back. I hope you do the same, son, and don't mess around. I'm talking about a breed of women whose men have let them down for so long, through many centuries, and dozens of generations, that they may be incapable of feeling pity for us, like almost everyone else does. They, more than anyone, it seems, accept that talk is cheap. Haitian men, we talk, boy, we talk. Son, you might be all right with them if you were born without the gab gene, son. If you unfortunately have that tendency, keep it in check. Park it somewhere. Don't be no talker, kid. Haitian women can love us still, and their love is . . . something else. Out of this world. Become a man of courage and substance, a doer, an earner, a creator of value in your life, in the world you live in, to match these women's character, son. That's my most fervent wish for you.

Listening to Philippe talk about his developing bond with Fabby, after weeks of watching Philippe lie, steal, and cheat to feed and nurse a thousand wounded strangers, Alain thought that if ever there was a Haitian man of substance worthy of the mythical Haitian woman of his dad's imagination, Philippe was one.

Philippe and Fabby's conversations, according to Philippe, were deep, their philosophies, ethics, and dreams were in sync and bullish. Their childhoods and backgrounds were similar (Her father was carpenter! Mine was a construction foreman!) the amount of times they'd been in love, where each was during goudou-goudou (I was in a car! Her too!).

Fabby kept Philippe on a tight leash, and this turned him on even more. She let me touch her hand! Philippe said one night. The next night? We touched foreheads and whispered for an hour!

What? Alain said. Did you kiss her?

No, Philippe said. But I'm getting closer!

The man had gone nuts. The man was happy. The man was in love with a capital "L." He grinned ear to ear after every bit of infinitesimal progress in extracting warmth from Fabby. I didn't know much about Philippe, Alain thought. He was older than me. Maybe about thirty, could be more. He had lines on his face that suggested he'd seen things, and that he'd suffered a great deal in his life. His cheerfulness, however, made him seem like a teenager. Post-earthquake, I aged ten, twenty years. This guy may have gotten fifteen years younger. Philippe would hate to have himself described as a spiritual guide and healer, he was too modest for that, but that's what he was for Alain and everyone around him in Place Pigeon. In fact, Philippe had all the talents of a voodoo priest. Alain didn't know much about voodoo, except that he knew believers moved between voodoo and Catholicism all the time. Catholics had the big churches and visible symbols and Sundays. Voodoo had every other day of the week, and once you got past that business about *loas*, *bondye*, and speaking in tongues, its tenets were banal calls to fellowship and faith in the unseen like most religions.

Philippe did look good in red, the color of voodoo. On the wedding day, Alain watched him strut through Place Pigeon in a wicked red suit, fire-engine-red shoes gleaming. You could tell Philippe felt pimpish, shaking hands and drinking compliments from friends and strangers with florid smiles. Fabby wore the whitest sliver of a dress Alain had ever seen in his life, the dress was of a whiteness Alain had forgotten was capable of existing. Philippe had proposed marriage to Fabiola the night after she'd first made love to him. She accepted, and the ceremony was promptly scheduled for two days later, because in the brave new world they lived in since goudou-goudou, they understood that love shouldn't wait. Death wouldn't.

You got the rings? Philippe asked Alain as they prepared to head toward the nearby National Cathedral for the wedding ceremony.

Of course, Alain said.

You're not going to say anything about my suit?

It's nice, Hollywood chimed in.

It sure is red, Alain said. You look great, man.

Merci, mes frères, Philippe said.

Philippe had made Alain the best man of his wedding, probably the first such event in refugee camp history, and in true best man fashion, Alain Destiné tapped his pockets and realized, Oh shit, I lost the rings. Without betraying his alarm, he took leave of the guys to try to undo this mistake. Excuse me, fellas, he said. Nature's calling.

Alain was sure he'd forgotten the wedding rings in a bathroom stall. The bathroom was shared with ten thousand other men. The odds that the rings were still there were not good. Yet Alain found them right where he'd left them, sparkling and ready. He exhaled in relief and almost thanked God. Back outside the bathroom stall, three men greeted Alain. Two of them pointed pistols at his abdomen. Their gun-less leader was fat and amiably kept his hands in his pockets. He put an index finger on his lips and told Alain not make a false move. Alain recognized the two gunmen. They were part of the quartet of thieves that Hollywood had foiled on his first night. The fat guy in the middle was a new face.

My name is Bobo, he said. We mean no harm. We were sent here by a friend of yours. He wanted to make sure you get the best medical help possible for your injuries.

Funny, Alain said. I feel fine.

But your leg, sir.

Alain's leg was indeed getting worse. Walking hurt more than usual. And now that Alain had finally washed himself, the funny smell coming from his knee seemed more ominous. Gangrene, possibly. Like in "The Snows of Kilimanjaro."

Who's this friend of mine who sent you? Alain said, though he'd kind of guessed his benefactor-enemy's identity already. What's with the guns? Friends don't threaten to shoot friends where I'm from.

The guns are a simple precaution, sir. Your benefactor is an important man who would rather remain anonymous for the moment. Please come with us now. All will be explained to you in the car.

Is that so? Where would you be taking me for treatment?

Miami, sir.

Despite his common sense, Alain laughed in Bobo's face.

Jackson Memorial Hospital!

If that's the nicest hospital in Miami, then yes, sir, that would be correct.

I haven't been there in years. It is a nice hospital, but there are better ones. All right, Mr. . . . what did you say your name was again?

Bobo.

Bobo. Of course, Mr. Bobo. The leg is probably killing me, so I will happily take up your boss's generous offer for help. Besides, I could use a break from Haiti, and Miami is especially nice in the winter. But I can't leave with you right this moment.

Mr. Destiné. . . .

Don't get me wrong, Mr. . . .

Bobo.

Right. Bobo. Sorry, I'm terrible with names. I'm not being a smartass. It's just that I have an immediate engagement. See that man over there? Not the white man, though I'm sure your boys here recognize him. The man next to him, the one in the red suit. He is about to get married now, and I'm his best man.

A wedding? Here?

I know the refugee camp leaves something to be desired when it comes to glamorous occasions. The wedding will take place at the cathedral. Isn't that great?

But the cathedral was heavily damaged by goudou-goudou. Isn't holding a ceremony there dangerous?

Bobo, my man, isn't love dangerous anywhere? Look where it's got me!

Bobo almost smiled. His gunmen grinned.

Alain didn't know where the big balls he was displaying had come from. Was a death wish still lurking in his subconscious even though he was convinced the bonhomie of Place Pigeon had helped him out of his depression? He pressed on.

Fellas, I can't leave with you now, because my absence would draw a lot of attention your way, and I'm sure you don't want that. Around twenty thousand people are coming to the wedding. Basically everyone around you is invited. They would notice the absence of the best man. So here's what I propose: Why don't you guys come to the wedding with me as my guests? Afterwards, you can take me to the airport for a one-way trip to Miami. I could use a vacation. It is a one-way flight, isn't it?

I'm afraid so, Bobo said.

Perfect! Alain said. It's settled.

I have to double-check with my boss, but yes, I think this should work.

Have your boss meet us at the cathedral! He's invited too. And why not? We are going to celebrate the love of a man and woman before God. I have a feeling your boss is a fan of such events.

Bobo and the guys looked at Alain like he was nuts, then they looked at each other to confirm that, yes, the guy was crazy but not much of a threat or a flight risk. He could barely walk, much less run. *D'accord*, Bobo said.

Put those away then, Alain said, pointing to the guns. Come with me.

And come they did, following Alain to his tent, graciously accepting introductions to Philippe, Hollywood, and Xavier as acquaintances of Alain's who happened to be in the neighborhood. Xavier gave them the side-eye. He suspected something bad was going on. Xavier tossed Alain a look that said, I hope you know what you're doing, and Alain nodded yes, he did. Meanwhile, the fat guy, Bobo, was on a BlackBerry, typing furiously. His BlackBerry beeped right back, startling the big guy, who, in turn, startled everyone around him.

Everything all right? Hollywood asked Bobo.

Yes, he said. Looking at Alain, Bobo said, Our friend will indeed join the ceremony, by the way. He was in the neighborhood.

Briefly, a look of absolute terror passed across Alain Destiné's face.

Not far away, on the corner of rue Borgella and rue Montalais, the president of Haiti was fuming in a limousine. He was sitting still, not moving forward fast enough, something he'd grown to hate doing much of since goudou-goudou. Cedric, how much longer are we going to sit out here? he said to the driver. I'm not getting any younger, you know. His limousine had been stuck in traffic making the short drive from the Champ de Mars plaza to the National Cathedral for over an hour. The thick crowds filling the streets on this earthquake victims memorial day were indifferent to his plight, and the President began feeling like the car was some sort of prison cell. After all, he'd started the day by spending a couple of hours stuck in traffic on his way to the Champ de Mars from the airport to make an appearance at the national memorial services. Mass grief had drowned out his speech. The crowd gave the impression of barely noticing he had made one. All their eyes seemed closed; their thoughts were elsewhere. Singing. Watching God, not another piddling politician. No doubt they were busy visualizing their lost loved ones and their own places in heaven next to them. Elysium fields and all that. On the podium, he was meant to appear humble and at one with them, but he struggled. He seemed beside the point, and the feeling made him uncomfortable. Who prays for me? he thought. Who weeps for me, huh? I've been working hard days and nights for you all. While you've been on your knees praying for help and begging for handouts, I've been working my ass off trying to make the help and handouts possible. Not all of them, but some of them. Most of them. It was difficult, lonely work. But gratitude rarely came his way. Not this day. And not ever, really. For not even his cabinet—kids he practically parented— could bring themselves to say Good job, Mr. President. Thank you, sir. No, all they could do after he walked out of one of those endless, if successful, meetings with narcissistic foreigners, feckless local businessmen, over-bearing journalists, and angry mayors, begging for aid, patience, coordination, generosity, and communality, was give him a look that said, If that's the best you can do, it's not enough, but we'll make do. Then they went about their business. They moved on to the next item on their agenda for him. Sitting in the backseat of a car that should feel good, since it was air-conditioned and the heat outside was no joke, the President shook his head. You should feel

better about your lot, man. Why can't you? This is your
finest hour as a human being and a public servant, and
you can't appreciate it. Your wife will. She gets your challenges. She gets you. She gets how much you love your
people, and how hard you work for them. Journalists who
cozy up to you claim they get it, swear they get it, occasionally report about it like they get it. But they don't get
it. How can they? How can they understand what its like
to be a leader who constantly has to negotiate on behalf of
a resource-free yet proud people with the resourceful and
haughty? Heads, you lose. Tails, you lose. Scientifically
anyway. As my beloved Natasha helped me see, my job is
an art, not a science, and in art, you are never wrong, you
never lose, your existence makes you a winner, your work
is victory herself. Sure, there was a marketplace, and there
were critics—where aren't there critics?—and reputations
could be constructed and made golden, and golden reputations unspooled purse strings, but the artist was never
wrong; neither was she often right; but that was not the
point of art, art existed in a place beyond right or wrong,
rich or poor; so does life, for that matter, in many ways,
if the Bible or Haitian history is to be believed. The point
of art, as Natasha saw it, in music, poetry, painting, sculpture, architecture, literature, film, was to be there. To exist. To have been born and held. To have been nursed and
breast-fed.

Man, I can't wait to see that girl again, the President
thought. It's been too long.

Outside, above his car, the brilliant sun howled. Lycée Pétion, his alma mater, stood near. His parents getting him into that school was one of the first great miracles of his life. He was glad the school was still standing after goudou-goudou and could soon become functional again. Its fortunes were better than that of its old rival, College Bird, down on nearby rue du Centre. That esteemed school's walls had been cracked throughout its skeleton by goudou-goudou. Its thick white columns seemed one good breeze away from tumbling onto themselves. Who knew how long it would take for that place to become safe enough for innocent students in their checkered yellow-and-white-and-blue uniforms to prowl its halls again? Bobo had told the President to come to meet them at the National Cathedral because his problems with Natasha were solved. The President saw their coming reunion this afternoon as an opportunity to renew their relationship with each other in front of God, a sort of renewal of their vows.

Cedric, I'm going to walk, the President said.

The heat was mean. The crowd around the cathedral was stiff, probably too hurly-burly for UN security protocols regarding the President's safety. He didn't care. Nobody noticed him. He looked up to the towers of the cathedral and used them as a beacon while threading along the potholed pavement with the masses. From their chatter, the President learned a wedding was about to take place in the cathedral. A popular young man from a refugee camp was about to take his first bride, the first marriage anyone could remember happening in Port-au-Prince since the earthquake. What an amazing thing indeed, the President thought.

Around the same time, on the other side of the cathedral, Alain Destiné walked behind the soon-to-be married couple in a procession from Camp Pigeon. All the procession had to do was cross rue St. Laurent. The street was clogged with people. Alain thought he even saw a TV news truck. Curiosity seekers joined the proper wedding guests from Place Pigeon. They wanted to know who was getting married and why now. There was a sense that Philippe and Fabby were a bit *oser* to dare something as romantic as a marriage at a time when death and grief and embittering shock dominated conversation about Haiti in Haiti and off the island. Alain's head was spinning. A spell of dizziness made the back of the heads of the lovers in front of him look like brown trees swaying between a molten sun in a hurricane. Just ahead the cathedral reared up as a final destination for the lovers, and the way things seemed to be going, the National Cathedral of Haiti could become Alain's final resting place too. Two goons kept the barrels of their guns pointed into Alain's lower back. This had the effect of making Alain walk on his tiptoes and feel like a man on a skewer. On his right, Hollywood Steve looked solemn, a look more appropriate for a funeral than a wedding. Maybe he didn't want a stray television camera or cell phone to capture how happy he felt. He loved weddings. I can't wait to get married again, he'd said more than once over dinner with Philippe and Fabby the previous evening. They were an inspiring pair. The couple was so in love, they looked invincible. On Alain's right, little Xavier walked with his typically preternatural calm, gazing into the distance. Alain kept a hand on the kid's shoulder, ostensibly so as not to lose the little guy in the surging crowds. In reality, he held on to Xavier for dear life, having long been seduced by the child's talismanic presence. He regretted having lied to the boy earlier. He did not have a plan for getting himself out of the jam he was obviously in with these goons. He planned a Hail Mary. He was going to bet that no one could be mad enough to kill someone in a cathedral, not even a justifiably jealous husband and his yes-men. Alain smiled at the irony of an atheist like him hoping the depth of others' faith in God would save his life. Such was the way of all atheists, he thought. No one's an atheist in a foxhole, his NYU buddy Alex used to say.

Hey, where's my best man? Philippe said, looking behind him for Alain.

Right here!

Swiftly, Alain bounded to his friend's side, forcing the gunmen to hide their weapons.

At your service, he said.

In his red top hat and suit lined with sweat from the long walk in the late afternoon, Philippe glistened. He wore a pensive frown and told Alain that his fiancée felt nervous about the crowds at the church's entrance. She worried whether the ceremony would start on time. The priest was a patient one, but he was old and sick. Say no more, Alain said. He took Fabby and Philippe by the hand and paused. Are you ready? he said.

Yes, they said.

Let's go then.

Alain raised an elbow to knife through the crowd, a trick learned a dozen Carnivals ago. Excuse me! he said. Coming through! Coming through! The crowd parted. *Pardon!* The friends charged the barricades of rubble blocking their way into the cathedral.

They ran, they giggled. The bride climbed a pile of rubble, then threw her flimsy bouquet at Alain and herself at Philippe standing on the other side of the pile, inside the church. They were dreamers, like everyone else, everyone around them, on the streets, on the radio, on TV, like everyone who has ever looked to a church for respite or a skyscraper for work and a living. They all sought the same thing. Alain had thought he knew what miracle he was looking for all this time. When he saw her, he realized he'd had no idea. Natasha was standing in the room next to the altar in the bowels of the National Cathedral. She wore a nun's robe and stood next to Monsignor Dorélien, who was going to perform the ceremony while holding on to a cane for what seemed like dear life. Natasha saw him first and stared with awe. The smile he saw on her face mirrored the one, a ballooning flash of joy, he felt explode on his own. Natasha's alive! She's alive! ALIVE!

And healthy and beautiful and wearing the one robe Alain suspected Natasha had dreamed of wearing all her life, a secret dream he knew she held without her ever articulating it. He smiled broadly at her with his entire face and body, his eye crinkling him blind. She did the same thing too, smile like a loon. Few people had ever seen Natasha Robert flash her full-blown toothy smile, and very few people had ever seen a young nun, in her nun robe, in a packed cathedral, abruptly stop nunning around to gasp and squeal, yes, squeal, at the sight of a young man. Alain swung Philippe and Fabiola toward Monsignor Dorélien—actually it was more like he flung them to the priest. They were practically airborne when they reached the front of the altar, and then, and then, and then, Natasha ran toward Alain, and Alain ran toward Natasha. Monsignor Dorélien looked up and said, Oh? Sister Hopstaken said, What? The crowd saw the young nun and the limping young man in the black suit hug each other with all their strength. They smashed into each other like atoms and they held each other tightly, tears running down their round cheeks. There was a tenderness to their embrace, a familial affection, onlookers were puzzled at first but they got it. They must be brother and sister. They must have thought each had died during goudou-goudou. Those types of reunions had been happening a lot all over Haiti since goudou-goudou. They didn't make headlines, but they happened, and they were wonderful to behold. Some onlookers sensed that the electricity between the striking nun and the skinny man had carnal roots. Those particularly sharp onlookers included the president of the republic, the nun's husband, and Monsignor Dorélien, the man who had led the nun through the Eucharistic gauntlet. The priest fixed the politician in the eyes and told him to be cool. Wait, he suggested, until he saw what happened next. What happened next was the squealing nun peeled herself off the handsome young man and touched his face and told him, I'm so happy you're alive.

Me too, the young man said, and then the nun, composing herself with ceremonial solemnity, took a step back and said, I must return to work now. I hope you understand.

Surprise registered on the young man's face, but then so did respect and love, so he said, I understand. Go do your thing. You look great.

Thank you, she said. You should take these.

Natasha gave Alain the keys to her car. It's yellow and parked out in the back, she said. I saw Villard and Katherine earlier. They really can't wait to see you.

Thanks, Alain said, then he, too, took a step back.

Natasha gave the President, who was standing nearby, an apologetic look. She bowed nervously and showed him her nun's robe. He shook his head in amazement. Natasha summoned the warmth and resolve of Sister Robert and walked up to her soon-to-be ex-husband and whispered in his ear. In this robe and in this line of work, she said, I can best help you take care of our people moving forward.

Your courage after the quake inspired me. You can retire in peace now, Jean. You did good. It's my turn. My work has just begun.

The President shivered. No one had called him by his given name in a long, long time. Her tenderness moved him. So did her determination. He nodded his approval and said good-bye. *Bonne chance*, he said. *On tient le contact?*

Bien sûr, Natasha said.

In the pink Haitian crepuscule, everyone in the rubbled cathedral took his or her appropriate place, and the first wedding ceremony after the earthquake began. It went off without a hitch.

EPILOGUE

Eights months later, a thin child was born in Miami. The earthquake taught us to expect the unexpected in life, didn't it? her mother told the child's ebullient father, Alain Destiné, adding, He seemed to have decided that you deserved a parting gift. The father named the baby Phoenix. Her uncle Jean called her Rose after the Alan Cavé song. Yes, the name of this child conceived in Haiti and born nine months after the devastating Haitian earthquake was Rose Phoenix Destiné. Her American friends called her Nicky. Nicky grew into a thin woman who didn't know much about her mother. She learned her father had lost the bottom of his right leg in a great earthquake in Haiti and was led to believe her mother disappeared around then too. Her grandfather and her grandmother from her father's side visited from Port-au-Prince frequently to shower her with gifts. Like clockwork, every other weekend, even after she moved to New

York City and then Paris to study art, Nicky had another visitor from Haiti, an aunty, her mother's twin, her father said. The nun ostensibly came to teach Nicky catechism and art. After Nicky became a successful artist in her own right and settled down in Miami, the nun continued to visit her regularly. By then they didn't talk art or religion much anymore. They took long walks and hung out on Lincoln Road. At night, they laughed at her father's attempts at cooking Haitian cuisine. The day he died, Nicky lamented she was completely alone in the world, an orphan. The kindly nun squeezed her hand and said, Not as long as I'm alive. Natasha then told her daughter the story of the love triangle and the disaster that surprisingly made everything right. All Nicky appreciated from the secret history of her parents was that, finally, she had someone on earth she could call maman. Like her mother, she hated to be alone.

ACKNOWLEDGMENTS

Heartfelt thanks, for their support through the journey to publication, to my agent, Robert Guinsler; my editor, Tracy Sherrod Fumi, and the team at Amistad and HarperCollins; and Edwidge Danticat; Junot Díaz; Madison Smartt Bell; Andrea Lee; Gary Shteyngart; Dany Laferrière; my sister Yanick Léger; my big brother, Elias "Tilou" Léger, and his wife, Marie; my kid brother, Steve; uncle George Clervoix and his family; Tisha Shea Harty; Tjade Graves; Adam Bradley; Kelvin Bias; Jason Liu; Stéphane Vincent; Marvin Barksdale; Christian Provencher; Ken and Rebecca Kurson; Daniel Loedel; Geoff Shandler; and Chloe Tattanelli and her family in Florence. In Geneva: Anthony Nguyen; Linden Morrison; Marcus Brown; Fran Costello; Frédéric Savioz. In France: Marvin Agustus and Vanessa Huguenin; Dominic and Lauren Waughray; Mirjam Schoening and Henrik Naujoks; and Fabrice and Elisabeth David.

ABOUT THE AUTHOR

DIMITRY ELIAS LÉGER was born in 1971 in Port-au-Prince, Haiti. Educated at St. John's University and Harvard Kennedy School of Government, he is a former staff writer at the *Miami Herald*, *Fortune* magazine, and the *Source* magazine, the seminal hip-hop monthly, and also a contributor to the *New York Times*, *Newsweek*, and the *Face* magazine in the UK. In 2010, he worked as an advisor to the United Nations' disaster recovery operations in Haiti after an earthquake. *God Loves Haiti* is his first novel. He lives between France and the United States with his family.